"You look sensational,"
Ha—he—sid Maggie.

outfit is okay for
an change . . ." His
just above the elbows,
burning brands into her arms, and suddenly she
wanted very badly for him to approve.

"You're perfect, except for one thing." He
reached into his pocket and produced a slim gold
wedding band. Then he took her hand, drew in a
breath, and slipped it onto her finger. "How does
it feel?"

No amount of warning could have prepared
her for the moment. Now she was overwhelmed
with emotion, and a sense of dismay that the ring
wasn't for real. "It feels a little strange."

He heard the catch in her voice and hurt for
Maggie. He wanted to tell her that it wasn't a
scam any longer, that he'd fallen in love with her,
but she'd never believe him. They'd known each
other such a short time. In a sudden move, he
took hold of her shoulders, backed her against the
wall, and kissed her. He liked feeling the woman
beneath the silk, the way she stiffened in surprise
then turned warm and pliant in his arms. He
kissed the pulse point on her neck and knew he'd
made her heart trip.

Maggie was trembling when he released her at
last. "Why did you kiss me?"

Books by Janet Evanovich

Wife for Hire
Motor Mouth
Metro Girl

Thanksgiving
Smitten
Manhunt
Back to the Bedroom
Love Overboard
The Rocky Road to Romance

One for the Money
Two for the Dough
Three to Get Deadly
Four to Score
High Five
Hot Six
Seven Up
Hard Eight
Visions of Sugar Plums
To the Nines
Ten Big Ones
Eleven on Top
Twelve Big Ones
Lean Mean Thirteen

Coming Soon in Paperback

Naughty Neighbor

JANET EVANOVICH

Wife for Hire

HARPER

An Imprint of HarperCollinsPublishers

This book was originally published as a Loveswept paperback in 1990, in a slightly altered form, by Bantam Books, a division of Bantam Doubleday Dell Publishing Group, Inc.

HARPER

An Imprint of HarperCollins*Publishers*
10 East 53rd Street
New York, New York 10022-5299

Copyright © 1990, 2007 by Evanovich, Inc.
Back cover author photo by Deborah Feingold Photography
ISBN: 978-0-06-059888-4
ISBN-10: 0-06-059888-3

First Harper paperback printing: November 2007

HarperCollins® and Harper® are registered trademarks of HarperCollins Publishers.

Printed in the United States of America

Visit Harper paperbacks on the World Wide Web at
www.harpercollins.com

10 9 8 7 6 5 4 3 2 1

Chapter 1

At the turn of the century the Bigmount Brick Company hired new arrivals from Eastern Europe to work in the New Jersey clay pits. The immigrants settled in the company town of Bigmount, and in the neighboring town of Riverside, building modest brick and frame houses on small lots. They kept their streets and windows clean, built bars on every corner, and poured time and money into the construction of their churches. Five generations later the population had been Americanized somewhat, but Riverside was still a blue-collar town with clean windows. The Russian Orthodox women still brought their bread to the church to be blessed, and the Polish National Hall was still booking weddings.

Ever since Maggie Toone was a little girl she'd wanted to hold her wedding reception in the

Polish National Hall. The country club in Jamesburg was prettier and any number of area restaurants more comfortable, but the PNA Hall had a paste wax dance floor that was smooth and dusty. It whispered during the slow numbers and thumped like a heartbeat when the stout ladies came out to polka. The hall was a place for weddings, Christmas parties, and silver anniversaries. It was as much a part of Maggie's childhood as braids, cream of tomato soup, and the sound of the freight train clattering through town in the middle of the night.

Over the years the hall had lost none of its appeal to Maggie. She couldn't say the same about marriage. It wasn't that she was against the institution . . . it was more that she didn't have time to seek it out. Finding a husband seemed like a real pain in the neck. Especially now that her life was at a crossroads.

She sat at the head of the picnic table staring at the chocolate cake. She gave a silent groan. It was the beginning of July and it was ninety-two degrees, and the cake was ablaze with twenty-seven candles and one for good luck. The candles were melting the frosting. Molten candle wax slithered in red, yellow, and blue streams across the top of the cake, spilling over the sides and collecting in small pools on the cake plate.

Ordinarily Maggie loved birthday parties—especially hers—but today she had other things on her mind, so she took a deep breath and blew the candles out without further ceremony.

"Isn't this nice?" Maggie's mother, Mabel, said. "A perfect day for a birthday picnic." She'd made tuna salad and deviled eggs and bought little dinner rolls from the bakery on Ferry Street. She'd even cut the radishes to look like flowers. "Did you make a wish, dear?"

"Yes. I made a wish."

"You didn't wish something crazy, did you?"

Maggie felt her left eye start to twitch. She put her finger on it to halt the tic and answered her mother. "Of course my wish was crazy. I wouldn't want to disappoint you and Aunt Marvina."

She smiled because it was a family joke. Her mother and Aunt Marvina rolled their eyes and sighed to each other because that's what they always did when Maggie made a joke about her craziness.

She was a problem child. Always had been. Always would be. It didn't matter that she was twenty-seven years old today, she was a continuing source of frustration to her family. She was a throwback to her flamboyant Irish grandfather—the only Irishman in Riverside.

"Twenty-seven years," Aunt Marvina said. "Where did the time go? I remember when she was a baby."

Mabel cut into the cake. "Even when she was a baby she had a mind of her own."

"She wouldn't eat her green beans," Aunt Marvina said. "Remember that?"

Mabel shook her head. "It's the green beans all over again. No matter what's good for her, she does what she wants anyway."

Aunt Marvina waved her fork. "When Maggie was nine years old, I told you she would never get married. She was such a tomboy. Was I right? Was I right?"

"You were right. She should have married that nice Larry Burlew. Or Jimmy Molnar. He would have married her." Mabel stared at her daughter who was pouring coffee at the opposite end of the picnic table. "Now she's quit her job. How is she going to live with no man and no job? Six years of college. A master's degree. For what? Two years of teaching down the drain."

Maggie's eye was twitching worse than ever. She'd spent too many afternoons with her mother and Aunt Marvina, she thought. If she heard about the green beans one more time, she'd start screaming. And Larry Burlew was a slug. She'd join the Foreign Legion before she'd marry Larry Burlew.

"She's always been stubborn," Mabel said. "Once she gets an idea into her head, there's no turning her around. So, tell me again," she said to her daughter. "Tell me why you're not going back to teaching this year."

Maggie helped herself to a second piece of cake. "I'm going to write a book," she said, picking congealed wax from the icing. "I'm going to write a book based on Aunt Kitty's diary."

There was more eye rolling from Mabel and Marvina. "That's craziness," Mabel said. "How are you going to live? How are you going to pay your rent?"

"I'm looking for a job that's not as demanding as teaching. Maybe something part-time that will allow me to spend most of my day writing. In fact, I have an interview this afternoon." She stared in amazement at her empty plate and wondered how she'd eaten that whole huge second piece. Even the wax was gone. She cracked her knuckles and cleared her throat, wondering if anyone would notice if she took thirds.

"So, what kind of job is this?" Mabel asked.

"It's going to be a wonderful book," Maggie said. "Aunt Kitty's diary is filled with information—"

Her mother wouldn't be distracted. "The job. I want to know about the job."

"This has been a terrific birthday luncheon, Mom and Aunt Marvina, and the cake was great, but I'm going to have to run." She was on her feet, with her purse slung over her shoulder, and her gifts tucked under her arm. She kissed her mother and gave her aunt a hug.

"The job," her mother insisted.

Maggie started off across the lawn to her car. "Nothing to worry about. Some man wants to hire a wife, and I'm meeting him for coffee at three-thirty."

She slid behind the wheel, slammed the door shut, locked it, rolled up the window, and turned the air-conditioning on full blast. She punched a CD into the CD player and looked back at her mother and Aunt Marvina. Their mouths were moving, but Maggie couldn't hear a word they were saying. She watched them for a moment, feeling the tension leaving her. Yes, even her eye felt a little better.

She smiled pleasantly, waved good-bye, and pulled out of the driveway.

She really was going to have to stop drinking coffee, Maggie thought. Her heart was jumping around in her chest, and she knew it couldn't have anything to do with the fact that the man sitting opposite her was drop-dead handsome. It had nothing to do with his soft, raspy voice or warm chocolate-brown eyes. Too much caffeine, plain and simple, no doubt about it. She pushed the cup away to avoid the temptation of one more sip, but she wasn't very good at avoiding temptation, so she pulled the coffee back and took another deep swallow.

Now that she was set to take on the role of wife, she gave one last wistful thought to the PNA Hall. "Do you think we should have some sort of party?" she asked Hank Mallone. "Do you think we should have a wedding reception?"

A look of shock registered on Mallone's face. He could barely afford the hamburger sitting in front of him, much less a fancy wedding reception. He didn't own a pair of black shoes, he hated pomp and ceremony, he didn't know how to dance, and most important of all, Maggie Toone wasn't at all what he wanted in a wife.

"No," he said flatly. "I don't think we should have a wedding reception."

Maggie gave a cursory glance to her surroundings. It wasn't a terrible restaurant, but it wasn't great either. It was only one step up from a fast food place. The plants hanging from the ceiling were real, and the floor was relatively clean. It could be worse, she decided. He could have taken her to Greasy Jake's for chili dogs. "It was just a thought," she said, smiling at him. "I love parties."

He caught himself smiling back and then immediately hardened his expression again. This was supposed to be a business luncheon. He was here to hire a wife, and he had very specific ideas on the subject. He'd told the employment agency he'd wanted a cool blonde with blue eyes and long sleek hair pinned in a chignon at the nape of her neck. His ideal wife would be sophisticated and reserved. She'd be the perfect hostess in a tailored suit or little black dress. She'd be someone he'd absolutely hate.

Maggie Toone was none of those things. She was devilishly cute with orange hair flying all over the place in tight little curls. She had a turned-up nose, snapping green eyes, and freckles everywhere. She was several inches shorter than the statuesque wife he'd ordered, and her voice was much too husky, her laugh far too infectious.

"I'm sorry, Miss Toone," he said, "but I'm afraid you're not exactly what I'm looking for."

"What are you looking for?"

"A blonde."

"I can be a blonde."

"Yes, but I wanted someone taller."

"I can be taller."

"Nothing personal," Hank said. "If I were in the market for a real wife, you'd be right up there at the top of the list, but I'm afraid you won't do for a fake wife. I need something different."

Maggie leaned forward, one elbow on the table. "Mr. Mallone, I don't know how to break it to you, but it's me or no one. I'm all the agency has. Nobody else is crazy enough to take a job as someone's wife and go move up to the boondocks of Vermont for six months."

"Are you kidding me? This is a great job. It's pretty in Vermont. There's free room and board and a salary on top of that. I've even hired a housekeeper." He looked at her closely. "If this is such a bad job, how come *you* want it? What's the matter with you?"

It was a question that caused Maggie a little confusion because deep down inside she harbored the same concern. What was the matter with her? Why wasn't she ever comfortable with the conventional? Aunt Marvina said Maggie did crazy things because she liked to attract attention. Maggie knew differently. She had never cared about the attention. She simply had different priorities.

She pushed her doubts aside and defiantly tipped her nose up a fraction of an inch. "I teach high school English, and I've taken a year's leave of absence to write a book. Vermont would be perfect for me."

Anything more than two hundred miles away from Riverside would be perfect, she thought. She loved her mother and father and Aunt Marvina, but she needed to get away from the little brick town with its winding streets and clay pit ponds.

She studied Hank Mallone and wondered if she was doing the right thing. His hair was dark, almost black, and a shade too long for the business mogul she'd been expecting. The employment agency had said he was chairman of the board of Mallone Enterprises, but he looked more like a model for a beer commercial. His eyes were overshadowed by thick black eyebrows and set deep into a tanned face. His nose was straight, his mouth was soft and sexy, his body was perfect—broad shoulders, slim hips, and a lot more muscles than she'd expected to find on a CEO.

"The employment agency said you were chairman of the board of Mallone Enterprises?"

The color in his face deepened. "I'm afraid they gilded the lily a little. I own Mallone Apple Orchards, and we have a factory that goes with it. Actually it's not a factory. We call it a factory because we don't have any real factories in Skogen, Vermont. Really it's just a big corrugated metal shed where Mrs. Moyer and the Smullen twins bake pies. Then we sell the pies at Big Irma's General Store."

This wife hiring had seemed like a good idea yesterday when he'd talked to the employment agency, but now that he was face-to-face with his prospective bride, Hank Mallone felt like a damned fool. Normal, intelligent men did not go around hiring wives. How could he possibly explain his reasons for needing an instant wife without sounding like an idiot? And the last thing he wanted was to sound like an idiot to the woman sitting across from him.

He'd wanted to hire someone he could easily ignore, but he'd ended up with a freckle-faced firecracker who had him thinking about sleeping arrangements. His scheme was doomed. If he took Maggie Toone home with him, she would make his life a living hell.

He briefly thought about trying another employment agency, but he knew it was too late. He was hooked. He wasn't sure exactly why, but he knew he was incapable of refusing anything to this adult version of Little Orphan Annie. If she wanted to go to Vermont to write a book, he'd move heaven and earth to get her there. He set his mouth in a grim line.

"So, what do you think, do you still want the job?"

She'd already decided she wanted the job, but she thought it wouldn't hurt to grill him a little.

"The employment agency said you simply wanted a woman-in-residence, and that I'd be expected to act as hostess once in a while?"

"Yup."

"Nothing else would be required of me?"

"Nope."

She gave him a long, considering look. If he wanted a wife so bad, why didn't the man simply fall in love and get married? It was a little suspicious. "What's the matter with you anyway? Are you weird?"

The color returned to his cheeks. "No. Jeez, I just need a wife for a few months!" He pushed his hand through his hair. "I want to expand my business, but none of the local banks will advance me any money. They say I'm not a stable member of the community."

She raised her eyebrows. "Why would they think that?"

"I was born in Skogen, but I took off as soon as I could read a road map. I'd played hockey all my life, and I was pretty good, so I tried going pro. I was this close to making it." He measured the air with his fingers.

"I was always good enough to get picked up in the draft, but never good enough to make final cuts. When that didn't work out, I bounced around for a while, trying to find something else that interested me. I guess I looked pretty shiftless to the folks in Skogen. Finally I decided to go back to school. I went to the University of

Vermont and studied agriculture and business, but I never graduated."

The grin he'd been holding back finally broke through. "Exams were always at the beginning of fishing season, or when there was good powder on Mt. Mansfield. It didn't seem right to waste good powder just to prove I knew something."

She nodded sympathetically; she'd often had similar sentiments.

"Most people think I have an irresponsible attitude," he said.

"I suppose it depends on what you want out of education. If you want the knowledge but don't need the grade, then you can go skiing at exam time. Of course I'd never stand for that baloney from one of *my* students."

"I didn't actually skip *all* my exams. We had a lot of rain for the first two years. Anyway, everybody in Skogen thought I was just wasting time and money, except for my Granny Mallone. She owned acres and acres of rolling fields that weren't being used for much of anything, and she let me come in and plant apple trees. I've got only one oar in the water, but I know there's a market out there for good organic food."

He forked in a mouthful of french fries. "My Granny Mallone died last year, and she left me her house and the orchards. The apple trees are finally maturing. I need to build a cider press and some sort of bottling plant, and I need a better facility for baking. I could eliminate almost all waste from my orchards if I produced more apple products."

"I think it sounds terrific, but I don't see what this has to do with me."

"You're going to make me look respectable, so I can get a loan to expand. You're going to get Linda Sue Newcombe off my back. And Holly Brown. And Jill Snyder . . ." He saw her mouth fall open. "I've had some bachelor ways," he explained. "But that's all in the past."

Maggie rolled her eyes.

"It's a small town," he said. "The people are fine, but they're stubborn, and it's damn hard to reshape opinion. I like growing apples, and I want to make a living at it, but I'm going to go down the drain if I don't get money from somewhere. I've been turned down for a loan once, but the bank has agreed to reconsider their position after the fall harvest. You help me look like I'm married and settled, and I'll help you write a book."

"Why don't you marry Linda Sue Newcombe or Holly Brown?"

Hank sighed and slouched back in his seat. "I don't love Linda Sue or Holly. I don't love Jill Snyder or Mary Lee Keene or Sandy Ross."

Maggie was beginning to feel peevish. "Just how many women have you had traipsing through your granny's house?"

He saw her wrinkle her nose in annoyance and heard the alarm bells go off in his bachelor brain. "You're not going to start making wife noises, are you?"

"Listen here, Hank Mallone. Don't you think for one minute you're going to go running after every skirt in Skogen while I sit home playing the pitiable wife. I have some pride, you know."

Yes sir, she was definitely going to make his life hell, Hank thought. She was going to sink her teeth into this wife thing. She was going to make him put down the lid on the toilet seat and stop putting empty milk cartons back in the refrigerator. And worse, she was going to tie him in knots. She was going to stand naked in his shower with a big Hands Off tattooed across her delicious bottom. She was going to show up for breakfast every morning in a

T-shirt and no bra, and his insides were going to turn to liquid. He had to be crazy to even consider this harebrained scheme.

"One more question," Maggie said. "Why did you come to New Jersey for a wife?"

"Last year I attended a six-week workshop on entomology at Rutgers. I figured I could say the romance started back then. And I'll be honest with you, I want someone who is far enough away not to be a burden or embarrassment when this arrangement is terminated."

"Lucky me."

Damn. Now she sounded mad. "No need to take it personally."

She sank her teeth into her burger, and chewed it vigorously. She didn't like being dumped into the possible burden category. It was practically implying that she would fall in love with him, or be a social buffoon.

"Why would you automatically assume your hired wife would be a burden or an embarrassment."

"It's just a worst-case scenario."

"Well, I can assure you, I won't be a burden or an embarrassment."

"Does that mean you still want to be my wife?"

"I suppose so. As long as I don't have to iron."

"I've hired a housekeeper. She's a little old, but she seems capable enough. She answered an ad I ran in a Philadelphia paper."

Now that it was settled, Maggie felt a rush of excitement. She was going to live in Vermont, and she would have time to write her book. Her eyelid had almost entirely stopped twitching, and the soles of her feet practically buzzed with the desire to get moving.

"When would you like me to start my wifely duties?"

"How soon can you get packed?"

She thought about it for a minute, calculating what had to be done. She had to notify utilities, the phone company, the newspaper boy. It might take a while to sublet her apartment, but she could put it in the hands of a realtor. "A week."

A week seemed like a long time to Hank. She could change her mind in a week. She could find another job. She could fall in love and get married to someone else. "I'm kind of in a rush to get a wife on board," he said. "Do you suppose we could shorten that to tomorrow?"

"Definitely not."

"You aren't one of those stubborn redheads, are you?"

She hated being called a stubborn redhead—mostly because she knew it was true. "I'm not a stubborn redhead," she said. "Tomorrow is totally unreasonable."

"Okay, day after tomorrow."

"I'll need three days minimum."

"Fine," Hank said. "Three days."

Chapter 2

It was raining when Maggie and Hank reached the Vermont state line at four in the afternoon. Two hours later Hank left the smooth superhighway running north-south and turned onto a secondary road. The secondary road quickly narrowed, winding its way around foothills, slicing into the heart of tiny towns and national forestland.

Water sluiced off the side of the shoulderless road, and rain ran in rivulets down the windshield of the old maroon pickup. Maggie anxiously squinted through the steamy windows, eager to take in all of Vermont.

It didn't matter that it was pouring buckets, that the sky was leaden, that the pastureland had been churned into viscous mud by the holsteins standing in small, sullen herds. It was all new and wonderful to her. No Markowitz

Coat Factory, no little brick houses with jalousies, no one watching from parted drapes to see what crazy Maggie Toone was up to.

"Are we almost there?" she shouted over the clattering engine and drone of rain on the roof.

"Two miles down this road and we'll be in Skogen. Then it's just three miles farther."

They hit a pothole and Maggie braced herself against the dashboard. "I think you need new shocks."

"I needed new shocks a year ago."

"And do you think the motor sounds funny?"

"Valves," he said. "The valves are shot."

"I should have brought my car."

"We've been all through that. You drive a sports car. No one's going to think you've turned me into a paragon of virtue and hard work when you go zooming around in a flashy red toy."

Houses stood back from the road with increasing regularity. They passed a forbidding yellow brick building labeled Skogen Elementary School, and suddenly they were rattling down Main Street with its large white clapboard houses and tidy lawns.

It was a classic New England town, dominated

by the Skogen Presbyterian Church, its white wooden spire punching heavenward through the rain. Big Irma's General Store was on the right, hunkering behind two gas pumps and a sign advertising live bait and fresh pies. Then came Keene Real Estate, Betty's Hair Salon, Skogen Sandwich Shop, Skogen First National Bank and Trust. That was the extent of the town.

The business district was left behind as the maroon truck pushed on. The land became more rolling, and the first of the apple trees appeared.

Hank turned into a private road that wound through the orchard. "You can't see the house from here because it's down in a hollow, but it's just past that hill ahead of us."

Maggie leaned forward and wiped at the windshield with the heel of her hand. She peered through the smeary circle she'd cleared, and gave a gasp of approval when the big white house came into view. It was just as she'd imagined. A gray slate roof, slick with rain, two stories of clapboard with lots of windows and a wide wraparound porch. A big black dog lay on the porch: Its head rose when the truck crept into the drive. Maggie could see the thick black tail begin a rhythmic thump on the wooden porch floor.

"That's Horatio," he said. "Man, it's good to be home!"

Maggie gripped the plastic cat carrier on her lap more firmly. "You didn't tell me about Horatio."

"We're buddies. We do everything together."

"He doesn't chase cats, does he?"

"Not to my knowledge." He had scared the bejesus out of a few rabbits, Hank thought. And once he caught a squirrel. But as far as he knew, Horatio didn't chase cats.

"Fluffy has always been an apartment cat," Maggie said. "She's never seen a dog. She's really a sweetie pie."

Hank gave the cat carrier a quick glance from the corner of his eye. Fluffy, the sweetie pie, was making unearthly growling sounds that had all the little hairs at the nape of his neck standing on end. "She sounds . . . annoyed."

"Don't worry," Maggie said into the cat carrier. "We're going to get you out of there right away. I'm going to take you into the house and feed you a nice smelly can of cat food."

By the time Hank had stopped the truck, Horatio was wagging his tail so hard his whole body was in motion. Hank opened the door, and the dog vaulted off the porch. He hit Hank at a flat-out run, planting two huge paws on Hank's chest. Both of them went down in the mud with a loud splat and a grunted expletive.

Maggie looked over and grimaced. "Are you okay?"

"Yeah," Hank said. He was spread-eagled on his back in six inches of brown muck. Horatio stood with his paws still on Hank's chest. "I'm just dandy."

She searched for something positive to say. "He sure seems happy to see you."

This is nothing, Hank thought. Wait until he gets a load of Fluffy.

"Is there anything I can do to help?"

The rain was pouring now and she had to shout to be heard. Hank was entirely soaked, and coffee-colored water was swilling around his pants' legs.

This had to be one of the worst ideas he'd ever had, Hank thought. He wondered if he rolled back onto his stomach and plunged his head into the puddle, would it be possible to drown himself? At the moment it seemed his most pleasant option.

He looked up into Horatio's face and took

solace. At least his dog thought he was wonderful. What Maggie Toone thought of him was beyond imagining. He definitely wasn't at his masculine best.

"Why don't you and Fluffy go on into the house, and I'll be along. The door should be open."

Maggie nodded and slipped out of the truck, clutching the animal crate. She moved as fast as she could, but she was drenched by the time she reached the porch. Rain dripped from the tip of her nose and off the ringlets at the side of her face. She removed her shoes and stepped into the foyer.

"Hello," she called, expecting the housekeeper he'd promised. But the house was dark and empty. A momentary stab of fear raced through her. What if there was no housekeeper? What if it had been a ploy to get a woman alone?

That was ridiculous, she told herself. The employment agency had thoroughly checked out Hank Mallone's background, and they'd assured her he didn't have a criminal record. Hank Mallone was exactly what he appeared to be, she told herself. But she wasn't sure that was comforting.

Hank stood at the bottom of the porch stairs

for a moment, letting the rain wash over him, removing the larger chunks of mud. He stepped under the protection of the porch roof, wiped the water from his face, and shook himself like a dog. He looked through the screen door at Maggie. Not a terrific homecoming, he thought. Her eyes were large, her lips pinched tightly together. He couldn't blame her if she was suddenly frightened and having second thoughts. He probably looked like some deranged yahoo.

"Don't worry," he said. "I'm not as stupid as I look. I couldn't possibly be."

"I'm not worried," she said, trying not to let her voice waiver. "I'm really very brave. One time I picked up a snake with a stick."

He felt a smile begin to spread to his face. Damned if she wasn't cute when she was trying to be brave.

"This is different," he said, waggling his eyebrows. "This is man-woman stuff. You're probably a little worried about being alone out here with such a smooth guy."

Maggie giggled. Ordinarily she wasn't the sort of person who giggled, but it gurgled from her throat in a rush of relief and gratitude. "Thanks. I guess I needed reassuring."

His gaze inadvertently dropped to her wet shirt, perfectly plastered to high, round breasts, and a pained look came over his face. Now if only he could reassure himself he wasn't a sex-starved pervert.

Because that's how he was feeling. He had mud in his ears, his briefs were waterlogged, and his shoes squished when he moved. Only a total degenerate could get aroused under those conditions, he told himself. And it wasn't just her shirt that was doing it. It was the way her eyelashes looked all spiky when they were wet, and the way the rain had brought out the scent of her shampoo.

"This is awkward," he said. "This is the first time I've ever pretended to be married."

He was so close, she could feel his body heat steaming off his rain-drenched clothes, and his nearness had the same effect on her as a belt of bourbon on an empty stomach. Fire roiled through her.

She took a step backward, and gave herself silent warning that she wasn't an impressionable teenager. Modern, intelligent women did not crumple into a heap of slavering goop just because an attractive man invaded their body space, she told herself. She gave his hand a motherly pat and made an effort to bring the moment back into its proper perspective.

"It's not so serious. It's a bogus marriage. It's temporary. I'll only be here for six months."

"Oh yeah? What if you get attached to me? Horatio was only supposed to be temporary. Big Irma asked me if I would take him for a few days, until she found a home for him. That was three years ago." He fondled the dog's satiny black head.

"Now he's crazy about me. I can't get rid of him. He follows me everywhere."

He leaned a little closer to her, and the corners of his mouth tipped up into a smile. "He'd do anything to get his ear scratched. *Anything!* That could happen to you, you know."

The man made a fast recovery, Maggie thought. One minute he was on his back in the mud, and the next minute he was teasing her.

"I'll try to control myself," Maggie said. "If I get a sudden, overwhelming urge to have you scratch behind my ears, I'll lock myself in my room."

Brave words coming from a woman who was already more than a little attracted to Hank

Mallone. Brave words coming from a woman who was having a hard time controlling her heartbeat because Mallone had moved a step closer and smiled at her.

She stood absolutely still, wondering if he was going to kiss her. Six months could be a long time if the relationship grew uncomfortable. And his track record wasn't encouraging. His past was littered with discarded female bodies. Her thoughts were interrupted by a loud droning noise drifting through the open door.

Horatio's ears perked up, and Hank turned to look outside. "Sounds like a car."

"Doesn't sound like any car I've ever heard," Maggie said.

The sound was low and throaty—a powerful motor guzzling gas through double carburetors, its life's breath resonating through a thirty-year-old exhaust system. It was a 1957 Cadillac, and it eased to a stop behind Hank's pickup.

"Looks like a little old lady," Maggie said.

Hank grinned at the Cadillac and the gray-haired woman behind the wheel. "That's no lady. That's my new housekeeper. That's Elsie Hawkins."

The woman jumped from the Cadillac into ankle-deep water. Her exclamation carried to the house, and Maggie burst out laughing. "You're right. She's no lady."

Elsie held an umbrella in one hand and a sack of groceries clutched to her chest. "Never fails," she said. "Just when you haven't got a crust of bread in the house, it decides to rain cats and dogs." She looked at Hank and shook her head. "You look awful. You look like you rolled in the cow pasture."

"A small mishap," Hank said. "This is Maggie Toone. I've hired her to be my wife."

Elsie made a disgusted sound. "Dumbest idea I ever heard of."

Hank unlaced his running shoes. "I agree, but I need that bank loan."

"I'm telling you there's more here than meets the eye," Elsie said. "Anybody can see you got a good business going. There's something fishy about your bank."

"They're just cautious." He peeled his socks from his feet and took the bag from Elsie. "I haven't led an exemplary life by Skogen standards."

"Don't sound so bad to me," Elsie said, following him into the kitchen. "It isn't like you've spent the last five years holding up convenience stores."

The kitchen was large and old-fashioned looking with oak cupboards and a big claw-footed table dead center. The appliances seemed adequate, but certainly not new. The room had a nice lived-in feeling, and Maggie could imagine generations of Mallones eating at the big round table. It was a kitchen that provoked images of little boys snitching cupcakes, and mothers and grandmothers working side by side to prepare holiday feasts.

"I got potato salad and cold fried chicken in the refrigerator," Elsie said. "You two can help yourselves. I got to get out of these wet shoes."

"So," Hank said to Maggie, "fried chicken or a hot shower and dry clothes?"

"No contest. I'm freezing. A hot shower sounds wonderful."

"I'll give you a quick tour en route to your room. Downstairs we have living room, dining room, powder room, kitchen. An addition has been added on to the original house. It was built as an in-law apartment when my Grandmother Sheridan came to live here after Grandfather Sheridan died. I've given it over to Elsie."

Hank skirted around the puddles in the

foyer and led the way upstairs. "There are four bedrooms up here. I'm in the master, and I've converted another into an office. That leaves two bedrooms for you. If you like, we can remove one of the beds and install a desk for your computer."

He motioned her into the larger of the two rooms. Their gazes met and held, and he felt his toes curling. Maggie had an energy that was refreshing. She was bright and funny and forgiving. Thank goodness for the forgiving part. He suspected in the next six months he was going to do a lot of things that needed forgiving.

"The bathroom's down the hall. Let me know if you need any help."

And you'd better lock the door, he thought, because he badly wanted to soap her back. He wanted to get her warm and relaxed and content.

Then he scolded himself. This was a bogus marriage. Fake bridegrooms don't get bathtub privileges. And decent men don't take advantage of women employees. The only question left to resolve was the extent of his decency. Ordinarily he liked to think of himself as an honorable person, but at the present moment he felt desperate enough to sacrifice a few principles.

"Help? What kind of help?" Maggie's stomach fluttered at the thought of all the possibilities.

He recognized the brief flash of panic that passed over her face. Great going, Mallone, he thought, you've succeeded in scaring her again. Nothing to be proud of, he admitted. He stuffed his hands into wet pockets and tried to make amends. "Extra towels, shampoo."

"Oh yeah. Thanks." Lord, what was wrong with her. She was far from naive, but she also wasn't the sort of woman who ordinarily saw innuendo everywhere. She preferred to take life at face value. It was much less complicated that way. Today she seemed to be reading sexual overtures into every move Hank Mallone made. It was because he excited her, she decided. Virility fairly spilled out of him. Even in his wet, bedraggled state he was sex incarnate.

He backed out of her room, feeling like a kid caught with his hand in the cookie jar, knowing he had a silly, embarrassed smile plastered across his mouth. "I'll get your suitcases from the back of the truck," he said. "I'll put them in your room."

Elsie's voice carried up from the foyer. "Well, what the devil is this? For goodness sakes, it's a cat. What are you doing locked up in this cage? Looks to me like somebody forgot to let you out."

Hank wheeled around at the sound of the latch being released. "Elsie, don't let the cat out while Horatio's in the house!"

"Don't Horatio like cats?" Elsie called up the stairs.

"I don't know!"

"Too late," Elsie said. "The cat's already out, and it don't look too happy about things."

There was a loud woof, followed by the sound of dog toenails looking for traction on the kitchen floor.

"Fluffy!" Maggie shouted, pushing past Hank to get to the stairs. "Poor Fluffy!"

The cat raced through the living room, into the dining room, and up the summer sheers on the bay window. It clung there with eyes as big as saucers, its tail bristled out like a bottle brush.

Hank, Maggie, and Horatio all reached the cat at the same time. Horatio took a snap at the tail. The cat hissed at the dog, catapulted itself onto Hank's chest and dug in.

"*Yeow!* Damn," Hank yelled. "Somebody do something!"

"It's the dog," Maggie said, trying to get between Hank and Horatio. "Fluffy's afraid of your dog."

Elsie snatched a piece of fried chicken from the refrigerator and threw it at Horatio. The dog thought about it for half a second and abandoned the cat for the chicken leg.

"Just look at this kitchen floor," Elsie said. "I just waxed it, and now it's full of scratch marks. I swear sometimes it doesn't pay to put yourself out."

Maggie was whispering soothing words to Fluffy, as one by one she pried the cat's claws out of Hank's chest. "I'm really sorry," she said to Hank. "Fluffy's never done anything like this before."

"It's had rabies shots, right?"

"Of course. *She's* had all her shots. I take good care of Fluffy." She removed the last claw and cuddled the cat. "I thought you said Horatio doesn't chase cats."

"I said I didn't know about him chasing any cats. Besides, Fluffy probably provoked him." Hank unbuttoned his shirt to examine the claw marks in his chest. "You ever check that cat's lineage? You ever find the name Cujo on the family tree?"

"Cujo was a dog."

"Technicality."

Maggie looked at the red welts rising over his hard, smooth muscles and felt a wave of nausea pass through her. His beautiful chest looked like a dart board, and it was her fault. She'd forgotten all about Fluffy, sitting not so patiently in the cat carrier. If she'd remembered to take Fluffy upstairs with her, this never would have happened. "Does it hurt?"

"Terribly. It's a good thing I'm so big and strong and brave."

"I'll keep Fluffy in my room for a couple days until she acclimates."

An hour later Maggie was sitting in the kitchen making her way through a mound of potato salad when Hank sauntered in fresh from his shower.

"How's your chest?"

"Good as new."

"I don't believe you."

He grinned at her. "Would you believe almost as good as new?" He took a plate of chicken from the refrigerator and dropped into a chair. "The rain is letting up."

"I hope it doesn't stop entirely. I love to fall asleep to the sound of rain on the roof."

"I like it best when it snows," he said. "The master bedroom is in the northeast corner and takes the brunt of the winter storms. When there's a blizzard, the wind drives the snow against the window with a tick, tick, tick sound. I always lie there and feel like a kid again, knowing the snow is piling up, school will be closed, and I'll be able to go out sledding all the next day."

"And do you still go out sledding?"

He laughed. "Of course."

It occurred to Maggie that she'd never sat across a kitchen table and shared small talk with a man whose hair was still damp. It was nice, she thought. It was one of those little rituals that was woven into the fabric of married life and gave comfort . . . like a good cup of coffee first thing in the morning or the fifteen-minute break to read the newspaper and sort through the day's mail.

Maggie watched the man sitting across from her, and a pleasurable emotion curled in her stomach. It would be easy to believe the marriage was real, easy to become used to this simple intimacy.

"I like your house," she said. "Has it always been in your family?"

"My Great-grandfather Mallone built it. He ran this place as a dairy farm. When my grandfather took over, he bought all the surrounding land he could and dedicated some of it to a pumpkin patch. He died ten years ago. My dad didn't want any part of farming, and Grandma couldn't manage the business by herself, so she stopped tending the pumpkins and kept only one cow. When I came back after college, I started planting trees where the pumpkins had once been."

"Do your parents live in Skogen?"

"My parents are the reason you're here. My father's president of Skogen National Bank and Trust."

"Your own father won't give you a loan?"

He slouched in his chair. "I was a problem child."

Maggie didn't know if she was amused or horrified. "Haven't your parents noticed you're all grown-up?"

"My mother thinks if I were all grown-up I'd be married. My father thinks if I were all grown-up I wouldn't have delusions of grandeur about growing organic apples."

His family and hers shared some disturbingly similar traits.

"This isn't fair," Maggie said. "It's one thing for you to be facing possible bankruptcy and ruin, it's quite another for you to be having the exact same problems that made me leave Riverside. I just spent half a day on the road to get away from my mother and Aunt Marvina, and now I find out your mother is blackmailing you to get married, and your father thinks your choice of lifework is ridiculous. I'm not going to have to get involved in any of this, am I?"

"Maybe a little. Mom and Dad are coming over for dinner tomorrow night."

Maggie stood so quickly, her chair tipped over and crashed to the floor. "What? No way. Uh-uh. Forget it. I barely know you. How am I going to convince them we're married?"

"No problem. I'm known for being impulsive and obstinate, and indulging in harebrained schemes. My parents will believe anything about me."

"What will I wear?" Even as she said it, she cringed at her classic female reply.

"Surely there must be something in all those boxes we packed in the back of the truck."

"Boring teacher's clothes."

"Good," he said. "That's great. Be a typical teacher. My mother will love it."

Maggie grimaced and wondered how to break the news to him. She'd been a good teacher, but she'd never been typical. She'd had a hard time sticking to the syllabus, sometimes her classes got a tad chaotic, and she didn't always have the patience to be diplomatic with parents. In the past two years she'd spent more time in the principal's office than Leo Kulesza, the only kid in the history of Riverside High School to repeat tenth grade four times. "What about food? I'm not the world's greatest cook."

"Elsie will take care of the food."

"Does Elsie know your father is the president of the bank?"

"Elsie arrived the day I left on my wife hunt. There wasn't much time for nonessential conversation." He lowered his voice. "Maybe we should wait until after the dinner party to tell her. Tact doesn't seem to be her strong suit."

"This isn't going to work."

"It has to work. I need that loan. I need it fast."

"Why don't you go to another bank to get a loan?"

"The banking community up here is very

small. I doubt if anyone would want to step on my dad's toes. And the truth is, I'm not all that solvent. I've already taken a mortgage on the farm to expand the orchards. Giving me another loan is going to be an act of faith. In all honesty, I can see my father's point of view. If I were in his position, I'm not sure I would loan me the money either. He has no way of knowing I'm capable of making a long-term commitment to a project. He told me to prove I could commit to something long-term; he told me to settle down and get married."

"What happens when I leave?"

He shrugged. "They'll have to deal with that." Just as he would, he thought grimly. "They're going to have to accept my failures as well as my successes. In the long run it's my opinion of myself that really counts anyway."

Maggie righted her chair. She took a chunk of potato salad and chewed it thoughtfully. He was no dummy. He had his ducks all in a row. He could be faulted for finding weird solutions to his problems, but he had strength of character. And that was a good thing for a husband to have.

Chapter 3

Maggie sat at her desk and stared, dreamy eyed, out the open window. There was a broad expanse of lawn, and after that there were rows of green-leaved apple trees stretching out over the low hills. The air was fragrant with smells of grass and earth, the sky was a brilliant, cloudless azure, the computer screen in front of her was blank, except for one phrase—"Once upon a time . . ."

Elsie knocked on the door and poked her head in. "You been up here for hours. What are you doing?"

"Watching apple trees grow."

"Aren't you supposed to be writing?"

"I'm getting inspired."

"Are you going to spend much more time at this inspired stuff? Hank's parents will be here in half an hour."

Maggie clapped a hand over her mouth. "I forgot!"

"Yeah, watching apple trees grow is pretty absorbing."

"It is, when you've spent your entire life in a town that makes bricks." She shut down the computer. "How's the dinner coming?"

"I'm not a fancy cooker, but my food won't kill anyone either."

"Good enough for me," Maggie said.

Twenty minutes later she swiped at her eyelashes with the mascara wand and decided she was as good as she was going to get. She wore a black-and-white zebra-striped silk shirt with a wide black leather belt and a little white linen skirt that rose an inch above her knees. She slipped her feet into black flats, posed once in front of the mirror and went flying from her room when she heard a car coming down the driveway. She almost collided with Hank in the hall.

"Whoa," he said. "Not so fast." He held her at arm's length and took a fast appraisal. "So, this is your boring teacher's clothes, huh?" A grin spread across his face. His mother was going to have a heart attack when she saw the zebra shirt and short skirt. He might have a heart attack, too, but for different reasons. "You look sensational."

"Do you really think this is okay? I can change . . ."

His hands were gripping her just above the elbows, burning brands into her arms, and suddenly she wanted very badly for him to approve.

"You're perfect. Except for one thing."

He reached into his pocket and produced a slim, gold wedding band. He held it between thumb and forefinger and studied it for a moment, feeling uncomfortable. He remembered his first real kiss with Joanie Karwatt. And some other more embarrassing moments. This ranked right up there with the most awkward pseudoromantic episodes, he decided.

He took her hand, sucked in some air, and slid the ring onto her finger. He realized he was holding his breath and released it with a loud whoosh, relieved that the deed was done. "How does it feel?"

Maggie looked at the ring and swallowed. No amount of warning would have prepared her for that moment. Only seconds ago she'd been filled with bravado, and now she was overwhelmed with strange emotions. Emotions she never even knew existed within her. It was with a sense of dismay that she stared at the band and realized it was only a front.

"It feels a little strange."

He heard the catch in her voice and hated himself. This scam had seemed so simple and harmless when he'd conceived of it a month ago, but now he was deceiving his parents. Worse than that, he was cheating Maggie. He wanted to tell her he loved her, but she'd never believe him. Hell, it seemed hard for him to believe. He'd known her such a short time.

He took hold of her shoulders, backed her against the wall, and kissed her. The kiss deepened, his hands moved to her throat and slid down her arms to settle at her waist. He liked the way he could feel the woman beneath the silk, liked the way she stiffened in surprise, then turned warm and pliant in his arms. He kissed the pulse point in her neck and knew he'd made her heart trip. The knowledge excited him, encouraged him. He knew he should stop, and he knew he wouldn't. Not just yet. He'd given her a ring. Now he was giving her a warning.

His hands took possession of the small of her back, crushing her closer, and his mouth moved over hers with a hard restlessness. He had a flash of self-directed censure. How would he ever step back from this? The answer was clear. He had no intention of stepping back.

Maggie sagged against the wall when he finally released her. Her fingers were tightly curled around his shirt material, her mouth ready to be kissed again, her eyes were heavy lidded.

She and Hank stared at each other for a long moment, trying to tidy up their emotions. She realized her fingers were still gripping his shirt and made an effort to straighten them. "Why did you kiss me?"

"Why?" Because it was all he'd been able to think about since the first moment he saw her. Unfortunately he couldn't tell her that. She'd think he'd hired her for all the wrong reasons— and she'd be right.

"Because I wanted you to feel married." At least it wasn't a total lie.

"Oh."

"Do you feel married?"

"Not exactly."

His hand curled around her neck. "Maybe we should take this a step farther."

She pushed him away. "No! No more kisses. We're getting wrinkled."

"Later?"

"No. Not later. Not ever. This is a business arrangement. Kissing and fondling aren't part of the deal."

His eyes narrowed slightly. "We could renegotiate the contract. I could pick up your medical coverage, contribute to your retirement fund—"

"No!"

"Okay, I'll throw in all the apples you can eat, and I'll increase your salary by ten bucks a week. That's my last offer."

"Ten dollars? You think my kissing is only worth ten dollars a week?"

He grinned down at her. "What do you usually get?"

She had a brief desire to kick him in the shins, but restrained herself.

"Very funny. We'll see how hard you're laughing when your parents get here."

Ten minutes later they were all settled in the living room and no one was laughing, especially not Hank.

"We've already been married," he said. "I don't want another wedding."

"It would be a reaffirmation of your vows," his mother said.

She was a large-boned woman with short-cropped salt-and-pepper hair. Her makeup was tasteful, her clothes tailored and impeccable, her shoes were sensible. Maggie instantly liked her. She was a no-nonsense, up-front person. If she had been a weaker woman, she probably would have been driven to drink by her maverick son. As it was, she looked like she had survived nicely. She was clearly relieved to have Hank married, but obviously disappointed that he hadn't had a more formal ceremony.

"And afterward we could have a party for you at the house. Wouldn't that be nice?"

Hank slouched in the rose wing chair. "I appreciate the offer, but I don't want to reaffirm my vows. They're still fresh in my mind. And Maggie here isn't much for parties. She's just a little homebody, aren't you, cupcake?"

Maggie felt her mouth drop open. Cupcake? "That's me. Just a little homebody," she said.

Harry Mallone looked at his new daughter-in-law. "Hank tells me you're a writer."

Harry Mallone was about as different from his son as any two men could be, Maggie thought. The elder Mallone was a solid man, thickening with age. His shirt was starched and freshly ironed, his striped tie perfectly knotted, his wing tips were polished. His posture was straight, clearly that of a man used to exercising authority. He was precise. He was consistent. He was cautious.

On the other hand, Maggie doubted Hank owned a tie. And caution wasn't exactly Hank's middle name. Clearly there was affection between the two men, but it was also just as obvious that they drove each other crazy.

Maggie nodded. "Two years ago my great-aunt Kitty Toone died and left me her diary. She wanted someone to use it as the basis for a book, and I suppose she thought I was the logical person, since I was an English teacher."

"How lovely," Helen Mallone said.

Maggie moved forward in her seat. "It's a wonderful story. My Aunt Kitty was a fascinating woman. I've been doing some additional research, and I have a detailed outline drawn up. Now all I have to do is write the book."

The very thought of it sent a thrill of excitement racing through her. It was accompanied by sheer terror. She hadn't any idea if she could pull it off.

"What sort of book will this be?" Helen wanted to know. "Will it be a romance? Will it be a sort of cookbook? I once knew a woman who wrote recipes in her diary."

Maggie thought about it for a moment. "I don't recall any recipes. My Aunt Kitty was a working woman. This will be primarily a chronology of her life and her business."

"A business woman," Harry Mallone said, "that sounds interesting. What kind of business?"

Maggie smiled and looked Harry straight in the eye. "Aunt Kitty was a madam."

Silence.

"Anyone want a cheeseball?" Elsie said, entering the room. "What's everyone so quiet about? You look like you just swallowed your tongue. What's the matter, don't you like cheeseballs? I made them myself. Got the recipe from one of them gourmet magazines."

Hank sent Maggie a tight-lipped smile. "Could I see you in the kitchen for a minute, Muffin."

"I thought I was Cupcake."

He jerked his thumb in the general direction of the kitchen and made a vague sound in the back of his throat. When they were behind closed doors, he smacked his forehead with the heel of his hand.

"Why me? What did I do to deserve this? All those women in New Jersey and I have to get one that's writing a porno story!"

Maggie stuffed her hands onto her hips and glared at him. "It's not a porno story."

"Honey, you're writing a book about a flesh peddler!"

"I'm writing a book about a woman who played a role in an immigrant community. She raised a child, bought one of the first refrigerators, turned her carriage house into a garage, and lived to see the Beatles on television."

"Are you telling me there's no sex in this book?"

"Of course there's going to be sex in it, but it's going to be of a historical nature. It's going to be high-quality sex."

"That's it. That's the ball game. That's the whole ball of wax. I'll never get the loan. The bank won't care how good the harvest is. I knew you were trouble from the minute I laid eyes on you."

"Oh yeah, well if I was so much trouble, why did you hire me?"

"It was you or nothing. You were the only one to apply."

They were standing toe-to-toe, nose-to-nose, hands on hips, shouting at each other.

"Fine. I'll un-apply. How do you like that? You can go find yourself a new wife."

"The hell I will. You made a deal and you're going to keep it."

He grabbed her by the shoulders and hauled her hard against him and kissed her.

Elsie barged through the swinging kitchen door. "What the devil's going on in here? You can hear the two of you shouting all the way to the living room."

She pulled up short and shook her head. "First you're yelling at each other like it's the end of the world, and now you're steaming up the kitchen. This arrangement isn't going to get weird, is it? I'm an old lady. I've got standards."

She went to the stove and lifted the lid on the cast-iron kettle. "This pot roast is going to be on the table in fifteen minutes, so you better hurry up and eat your fill of cheeseballs. And if you ask me, it wouldn't hurt to give those people in there something to drink. They look like they've been left in the starch too long."

Elsie was true to her word. In fifteen minutes

the pot roast was on the table, along with homemade buttermilk biscuits, mashed potatoes, cooked carrots, homemade applesauce, and steamed broccoli. She set a bowl of gravy on the table and took her apron off.

"There's a TV show coming on that I've got to watch," she said. "There's more potatoes in the kitchen and there's apple pie for dessert."

"Thanks, Elsie," Maggie said, "I can handle it from here."

Elsie looked the table over one last time, obviously reluctant to leave her food in Maggie's hands. "There's vanilla ice cream to go with the pie, and don't forget the coffee. It's all made."

"You sure you don't want to eat with us. There's room . . ."

"Nope. Thanks anyway. I'm not much for socializing. I got things to do. Just make sure everybody gets enough to eat, and watch the piece of pie you give to Harry. He's starting to spread."

There was a knock at the door and Elsie went to answer it. "It's Linda Sue Newcombe," she called from the foyer. "She says she got stood up for a date last night, and wants to know why."

Hank looked surprised. "I don't remember making a date."

Linda Sue stomped into the dining room. She was short and blond and steaming mad.

"You promised to take me to the dance at the grange. We made that date two months ago." She smiled a polite hello to Hank's parents. "Excuse me," she said to them, "but I bought a new dress for that dance."

Hank hated dances and doubted he'd agreed to go to this one. Linda Sue had a tendency to ramble, and he had a tendency to tune her out. He suspected he'd missed an important part of a conversation with her. It was a good thing he was married, he thought. His social life had become too complicated.

Linda Sue pouted a little and looked at Hank under lowered eyelashes. "Maybe you can make it up to me."

"I don't think so," Hank told her. "I got married last week."

Linda Sue's eyes snapped wide open. "Married?"

He gestured with a half-eaten biscuit. "This is my wife, Maggie. . . ."

Linda Sue had her hands on her hips. "You were going to marry me!"

Hank pressed his lips together. "I never said I was going to marry you. *You* said I was going to marry you."

"Would you like to join us for dinner?" Maggie asked. "We have lots of food."

Linda Sue looked at the pot roast. "It smells good. What are you having for dessert?"

"Apple pie and vanilla ice cream."

"Sure, I'll stay." She took a side chair and dragged it over to the table. "When Hank's granny lived here, I used to stay for dinner all the time. Hank's granny always had an extra potato in the pot for company."

Maggie set a place for Linda Sue. "Do you live near here?"

"I used to live just over the rise, down the road. My parents still live there." She helped herself to some pot roast.

Maggie waited for Linda Sue to continue, or someone else to make conversation, but Linda Sue's attention had been caught by the mashed potatoes and Hank's parents were staring out the window. Finally Maggie couldn't wait any longer. "Where do you live now?" she asked.

"I live in the Glenview apartments now. They're outside of town, just off the interstate to Burlington."

The doorbell rang again and Maggie excused herself to answer it.

"I'm Holly Brown," the woman said when Maggie opened the door. "Is Hank here?"

"He's in the dining room."

Holly Brown walked into the dining room, gave a slanty-eyed look to Linda Sue Newcombe and a large, wet kiss to Hank. She smiled at his parents and said hello.

"I heard you'd gotten back in town," Holly said to Hank. "Just thought I'd stop by to welcome you home."

"Save it," Linda Sue said. "He's married."

Holly gave a disbelieving snort. "Hank? Married?"

Maggie dragged out another set of dishes and silverware, making a place for Holly. "I'm Maggie," she said. "We were married last week. You'll stay for supper, won't you?"

"Sure you have enough?"

"Plenty," Maggie said. She knew it was ridiculous, but darned if she didn't feel like a real wife. She was feeling possessive, and jealous, and cranky. She glared at Hank.

"Is there anyone else we should be expecting? Maybe I should cook up more potatoes."

Holly Brown slung her purse over the back of

her chair and sat down. "This marriage is awful sudden."

Hank sliced his pot roast. "Maggie and I met last summer when I was at Rutgers."

Holly and Linda Sue exchanged glances. They looked skeptical.

"Still seems sudden to me," Holly repeated. "The entire female population of Skogen's been after Hank for years," she told Maggie. "He's as slippery as they come. Nothing personal, but it seems a little odd that he'd go to New Jersey and come back married."

"It was one of those things," Maggie said. "Love at first sight."

Holly poked around at the pot roast, looking for the end piece. "Honey, it's always love at first sight with Hank. It's never caused him to get married before."

Linda Sue poured more gravy over her potatoes.

"This house sure holds memories," Holly said. "When I was a little girl, my daddy worked for the co-op and he'd come collect the milk from all the local dairy farms. Sometimes, in the summer, he'd let me ride with him. Hank's granny always invited me in for cookies and lemonade. If Hank was here I'd stay and play

Monopoly with him on the front porch. Then when he got older—" She stopped in midsentence, cleared her throat, and concentrated on slicing her meat.

Linda Sue, Hank's mother, and Hank's father also cleared their throats and became totally absorbed in the process of eating.

Maggie looked sideways at Hank.

"Vern's dog ate my Monoploly set," Hank explained.

Linda Sue tilted her head toward Hank. "Does Bubba know you're married?"

"Not yet." Hank reached for another biscuit. "I haven't seen him since we got back."

"Bubba's not going to like this," Linda Sue said. "You should have told him."

"Who's Bubba?" Maggie asked.

Everyone but Hank looked shocked.

His mother was the first to find her voice. "Bubba has always been Hank's best friend. I'm surprised Hank didn't tell you about him."

There was the squeal of brakes on the driveway, and Horatio began barking.

"I guess it's my turn," Hank said. A moment later he returned with two middle-aged women.

Maggie grabbed the table for support. "Mom! Aunt Marvina!"

Maggie's mother gave Maggie a kiss. "We were in the neighborhood, so we thought we'd stop by and see how things were going."

In the neighborhood? It was a six-hour drive. Calm yourself, Maggie thought. This couldn't be as bad as it seemed. "Things are just fine. Aren't they fine, Hank?"

"Yup. They're fine."

"Mom, Aunt Marvina, I'd like you to meet Hank's mother and father, and this is Linda Sue, and this is Holly." Maggie set out two more plates and Hank brought chairs from the kitchen. "We were just explaining to Linda Sue and Holly how Hank and I met last summer while he was at Rutgers."

Holly stabbed a wedge of pot roast. "I think it seems awful sudden."

Mabel Toone and Aunt Marvina exchanged looks. "Just what we said," Mabel told Holly. "There wasn't even time to get the PNA Hall." She shook her finger at her daughter, but the scold was tempered by obvious affection. "You're such a problem child."

"When she was a baby, she would never eat her green beans," Aunt Marvina said. "She always had a mind of her own. It's from her Grandfather Toone. The only Irishman in Riverside, and I tell you he was a rascal."

Hank sat back in his seat and watched Maggie squirm. This wasn't doing his cause any good, but he was enjoying it anyway. And he had a thirst to know more.

"Maggie didn't tell me she was a problem child," Hank said. "In fact, Maggie hasn't told me much about her childhood at all."

Mabel rolled her eyes. "She was the terror of Riverside. Ever since she was a little girl, the boys loved her red hair. They just flocked to our doorstep, and Maggie wouldn't have anything to do with them." She shook her head. "She wasn't one to pussyfoot around. If they didn't take no for an answer, she'd punch them in the nose, or hit them over the head with her lunch box. When she got older, it was just as bad."

"We thought she'd never get married," Aunt Marvina said.

"And then, remember that time when she was nine," Mabel said, "and she wrote that awful word on the front door of Campbell School?"

Aunt Marvina clapped her hand to her mouth

to keep from laughing out loud. "That was terrible." She looked at Hank, her eyes crinkled at the memory. "We were surprised she even knew a word like that, but then Maggie was always surprising us."

"I wrote that word on a dare," Maggie said. "And I went back later to wash it off."

Mabel buttered a biscuit. "It wouldn't wash off," she told Hank. "They had to paint the door. And we had to pay for the paint."

Maggie's aunt was right. Maggie was full of surprises, Hank thought. It was easy to imagine her as the neighborhood tomboy. And she didn't seem to be so different now. She probably still punched men in the nose. Something he should keep in mind.

"So what else did Maggie do?"

Maggie glared a warning to Hank and her mother. "I'm sure everyone is finding this very boring."

"Not me," Linda Sue said.

Holly Brown sipped her water. "I want to know more."

"This is good pot roast," Mabel said. "And no lumps in the mashed potatoes. You see," she said to Aunt Marvina, "all she needed was to get married. Now she can even cook."

"Wrong," Maggie said. "I still can't cook. We have a housekeeper. She made the meal."

"A housekeeper." Mabel was clearly impressed. "That's very nice, but what will you do all day if you don't have to cook and clean?"

"I told you. I'm writing a book about Aunt Kitty."

Mabel sucked in some air. "A book about Aunt Kitty. That's craziness. Aunt Kitty was a . . . you know what. Why do you have to write a book that's filled with S-E-X? How will I ever be able to show my face at Wednesday night bingo?"

Linda Sue's eyebrows shot up under her bangs. "You're writing a dirty book?"

"My Great-aunt Kitty was a madam," Maggie explained to Linda Sue and Holly. "She left me her diary, and I'm using it as the basis for a book."

"Wow, hot stuff," Holly said. "This should put Skogen on the map."

Harry Mallone had turned a deep shade of vermilion. He had his hand wrapped around his fork and his knuckles were white. "Over my dead body," he said.

Helen Mallone patted her husband's hand. "Watch your blood pressure, Harry."

Maggie thought her mother-in-law didn't look especially concerned about Aunt Kitty's diary. Helen Mallone was amazingly calm. In fact, there was an unnerving peacefulness about her.

Helen caught Maggie staring. "I've survived Hank's adolesence," Helen explained. "The rest of my life will be child's play. And now he's your responsibility, dear." She sank back into her seat with a look of enviable serenity.

Hank grinned. "I wasn't that bad."

Linda Sue fanned herself with her napkin. "Honey, you were the scourge of Skogen."

Maggie's heart did a little tap dance. The scourge of Skogen? What sort of man was she living with? Sexy, she decided. Too sexy. She thought about the kiss in the upstairs hall and promised herself it wouldn't happen again. He was one of those men who collected women like other men collect stamps or coins. Two of his women were sitting at the table. Probably if she looked out the front window she'd see a hundred more camped out on the lawn.

She felt herself flush hot and looked over at Hank. He was watching her, and he was smiling. The scourge of Skogen knew when a woman was attracted to him, she thought. That was undoubtedly one of the things that made him such a scourge.

She took a deep breath, relaxed her shoulders, and sent Hank a warning smile. "All that's in the past," she said. "Hank's a married man. His scourging days are over. Isn't that right, dumpling?"

"That's right, sweetcakes," Hank said. "I do my scourging at home now."

Maggie felt the smile tighten on her face. This was going to be a long six months if she was going to have to ward off his scourging every day. She'd never put up with much from the male population of Riverside, but then she'd never been swept off her feet by any of them. No one had ever made the earth move when they kissed her. No one until Hank. It was going to be tough to resist the advances of a man who had the potential to fulfill every fantasy she'd ever had.

Helen Mallone turned to Maggie's mother. "Sounds like a marriage made in heaven."

"Yeah," Linda Sue said, "sounds like they deserve each other."

Maggie didn't think that sounded especially flattering.

"Goodness," Mabel said to Maggie, "you look

just like your Grandfather Toone when your eyes get all beady and glittery like that."

"It's true," Aunt Marvina said. "Your Grandfather Toone had a short fuse. If some poor soul was dumb enough to insult your Grandfather Toone, your Grandfather Toone would haul off and rearrange the man's face. He had some temper, didn't he, Mabel?"

Linda Sue's eyes got wide. "Holy cow," she said to Maggie, "you aren't a face rearranger like your grandfather, are you?"

"Don't worry about Maggie," Hank said to Linda Sue. "We decided now that she's a married woman she'd go easy on the violent stuff. She's even agreed to stop mud wrestling."

Holly's mouth fell open. "Do you really mud wrestle?"

"She was the best," Hank answered. "She was the Central Jersey Mud Wrestling Queen."

Maggie shot out of her seat. "Hank Mallone, I'd like to see you in the kitchen, please."

"She's got that look again," Linda Sue said. "I bet she's going to hit him."

Maggie swished through the kitchen door and closed it behind her. "Mud wrestling? *Mud wrestling?* Don't you think this dinner has gotten far enough out of hand?"

"I thought you'd be pleased. I told them you were the best."

She had him by the shirtfront. "This is serious!" she yelled. "Your parents think I'm a reformed mud wrestler!"

"Calm yourself," Hank said. "I've decided to make my parents think I've reformed you. Then they'll really think I'm stable." He massaged her shoulders. "You have to learn how to relax. Look at you . . . you're entirely too tense."

He was right, she realized. She *was* tense. And probably she'd overreacted. Certainly her mother and Aunt Marvina would set everyone straight. No one would seriously believe she was a mud wrestler. It was absurd.

"You're right," she said. "Silly me. Probably the dinner's going better than I think. Just because your father can't relax his grip on his fork is no reason to think things aren't going well."

"Exactly. My father's knuckles always turn white when he eats."

"And there are a lot of positive things to be said about this dinner party," she continued. "No one's gotten sick. No one's insisted we have the marriage annulled. That's a good sign, isn't it?"

"You couldn't ask for much more than that."

"And my mother hasn't even brought out my

baby pictures . . . the ones where I'm mashing green beans into my hair. She hasn't mentioned Larry Burlew or the time I had to stay after school for two weeks in the second grade for chewing gum. She hasn't told anybody about how I drove the Buick into Dailey's Pond or how I got locked in Greenfield's Department Store overnight."

She looked over her shoulder at the closed kitchen door. "Of course, it's still early. She's only just arrived." She chewed on her lower lip. "I should never have left the room. That's like an open invitation in Riverside. You leave the room and you're road kill."

Hank looked at her more closely. "Something wrong with your eyebrow?"

"Why do you ask?"

"It's twitching."

"Oh no! Oh, that's just great." She slapped her hand over half of her face. "Now on top of everything else your parents will know I'm a twitcher. Tell me the truth. Do you think this could get any worse?"

Aunt Marvina's voice carried in from the dining room. "For goodness sakes, it's Fluffy! And she's skulking around looking scared to death."

"Fluffy?" Hank and Maggie mouthed the word in unison.

Maggie groaned. "I must have left my bedroom door open." Her hand clamped back onto his shirtfront. "Horatio's outside, isn't he?"

"Horatio is under the dining room table."

There was a bloodcurdling cat screech, and Hank and Maggie rushed to the dining room. Fluffy was backed into a corner. Her ears were flat back to her head, and she growled low in her throat. It was a sound that would put fear into the heart of any living creature . . . with the possible exception of Horatio.

Horatio bounded up to the cat, gave a joyful bark and pinned the cat with one heavy paw. There was another feline growl, followed by a quick right claw to the snoot. Horatio yelped in pain and Fluffy took off, climbing up the first available object—Harry Mallone's rigid back.

Horatio snapped at the cat, and Fluffy hurled herself onto the table, knocking over a candlestick. In an instant the white linen tablecloth was a wall of flames. Hank grabbed a corner and yanked the tablecloth into the kitchen and through the back door, leaving a trail of singed food and broken crockery.

Everyone followed Hank outside and circled

the little bonfire of food and linen that was burning on the back lawn. Their eyes glazed over in rapt fascination and their jaws went slack in stupid silence as the buttermilk biscuits burned one by one, then the carrots and broccoli and, last but not least, the beef incinerated.

So this is what my first dinner party is reduced to, Maggie thought. A bunch of people standing around watching a rump roast burn. She had a ridiculous urge to sing camp songs and checked to see if anyone else was smiling. Only Hank was.

Their gazes caught and held, and Maggie felt her heart begin to beat faster. She couldn't remember a man ever looking at her quite that way. His mouth was smiling, but his eyes were hungry and possessive. There was a moment of perfect understanding, a meeting of minds and emotions, and an acknowledgment of genuine affection that passed between them.

Chapter 4

The rump roast got boring after a while. It had burned itself into a charred chunk about the size of a baseball. It was black enough to look like a Cajun delicacy and had the density of a meteorite.

"So," Maggie said, "anyone ready for dessert?"

"I think I'll pass," Linda Sue said. "I have to be getting on home now."

Holly tiptoed around the mashed potatoes on the back porch, following Linda Sue. "Yeah, me too. This has been great, but it's getting late."

Harry Mallone clamped a hand on his son's shoulder. It was a gesture of condolence usually reserved for sickrooms, wakes, and the passing on of a severance check.

Hank chose to ignore the obvious. "About that loan—"

Helen Mallone gave Maggie a hug. "I'm going to take Harry home now, and don't worry about the roast, dear. Hank never was much of one for leftovers. Maybe it's all worked out for the best," she said gently.

Elsie met Maggie in the kitchen. "Do I smell something burning?"

Maggie sniffed the air. "I think that's the pot roast. Fluffy knocked over a candlestick and the tablecloth caught fire. Hank dragged it all out into the backyard."

Elsie looked through the screen door at the smoldering rubbish. "It don't look so bad. You didn't burn down anything important. Is that black chunk the pot roast?"

"Yup."

"I've eaten worse," Elsie said.

Half an hour later the remains of the fire had been shoveled into a garbage bag, the floors were fresh scrubbed, and the unbroken dishes had been washed and dried. Mabel and Aunt Marvina, Elsie, Hank, and Maggie sat at the kitchen table, eating pie and ice cream.

"I remember my first party as a new bride," Mabel Toone said. "I'd only been married for three weeks and I had dinner for fourteen on Christmas Eve."

"I can see it like it was yesterday," Marvina said. "I wore that green velvet dress with the rhinestones on the bodice. Everything was perfect, except that Great-aunt Sophie had too much to drink and fell into the pineapple upside-down cake. Her elbow slipped off the table," Marvina explained, "and Sophie went face first into the whipped cream. It made a terrible mess."

"We didn't mean to interfere with *your* party," Mabel said to Maggie. "It's just that we were worried about you, so we came to check up."

"Mom, I'm twenty-seven years old. I can take care of myself."

"You left in such a hurry, and all you said was that you were going to live with this man in Vermont. We weren't even sure you were getting married. There's something fishy here. Are you . . . ?"

Maggie put her finger on her fluttering eyebrow. "No. I'm not pregnant."

Mabel Toone looked Hank over. "Did he force you into this? Did he kidnap you? He looks a little shifty to me."

"I wasn't kidnapped," Maggie said. "I needed a quiet place to write my book, and Hank sort of showed up . . ."

Mabel looked horrified. "You mean you got married so you could write a book?"

"Yes. No!" She didn't want her mother to worry about her. And she didn't want her mother to think she was an idiot. "I got married because . . . I wanted to."

Hank inched his chair closer to Maggie and slung his arm around her shoulders. "Love at first sight," he told Mabel. "As soon as we saw each other we knew this was it." He gave Maggie a big, loud kiss on the top of the head. "Go ahead, buttercup, tell your mother how much you love me."

"Uh . . . I love him lots."

Mabel didn't look convinced. "I don't know."

Hank loosened his hold on Maggie. His chin rested against the mass of orange curls over her ear, and his voice grew softer, more serious.

"I know this must be difficult for you, Mrs. Toone. You're worried about Maggie, and I don't blame you. We shouldn't have been so secretive about our romance, but the truth is, it sort of took us by surprise. I think it would be nice if you and Aunt Marvina could stay with us for a few days. I'd like the opportunity to get to know you better."

His fingertips lightly combed through the

wisps of hair at Maggie's temple, and a rush of tenderness for the woman he held in his arms almost left him breathless. "I love your daughter," he told Mabel Toone. "And I intend to take very, very good care of her."

"I guess a mother couldn't ask for more than that," Mabel said. "It's nice of you to invite us to stay, but we've got a room at one of those bed-and-breakfast places, and then we've got to get back to Riverside. Marvina has an appointment to get a permanent on Thursday, and nobody will water my plants. Besides," she said with a broad smile, "I know how it is with newlyweds."

Hank made a masculine sound of appreciation. It hummed against Maggie's ear, sending vibrations all the way to the soles of her feet. In spite of all her good resolve, she felt herself relax into him.

It was almost impossible not to like Hank Mallone. He might be a womanizer and a schemer, but he was also sensitive and charming and there was something about Hank Mallone that touched her. He didn't just heat her blood—he also warmed her soul. It was nice, and it was sad. And it was infuriating that he'd lied so smoothly about loving her. Hank Mallone was a rascal, she thought.

"Well," Mabel said, "we should be getting on. The pie was delicious," she said to Elsie. She gave her daughter a kiss and hugged her son-in-law. "You keep in touch."

"They're nice people," Hank said when he and Maggie were left alone on the front porch. "They really care about you."

He was being generous, Maggie decided. He could have said they were meddlesome. "You think I'm a bad daughter?"

He laughed. "No. I think you're struggling to find a balance between being a daughter and being an independent adult. And I think you're mother's struggling to relate to an adult child."

She looked thoughtful for a moment, then asked. "Do you think your father will give you the loan?"

"I don't know. He didn't look too happy when he left." He tugged at an orange curl. "I don't suppose you'd consider getting pregnant?"

"No. I don't suppose I would."

"Just checking."

* * *

Maggie was used to hearing cars leaving the parking lot first thing in the morning. She was used to the sound of the garbagemen emptying the dumpster, and to hearing old Mr. Kucharski's smoker's cough, as he shuffled overhead from bedroom to bathroom. They were sounds she'd always hated, and it surprised her to find that she missed them. She dragged herself out of bed, shrugged into a worn navy T-shirt and cutoff gray sweats, and padded barefoot to the kitchen, following the smell of fresh-made coffee.

Hank was already at the table. He looked up and groaned. His worst fears and best fantasies were coming home to roost. Maggie Toone was a vision of morning allure with her mussed hair and sleep-softened face. She poured herself a cup of coffee and immediately took a sip. She'd been about to say something, but the pleasure of that first sip of coffee erased all thought. Instead, she smiled and gave a contented sigh.

Elsie took a tray of homemade cinnamon rolls from the oven and knocked them out into a napkin-lined basket. "Don't think I'm going to do this every day," she said. "It's just that I felt like eating cinnamon buns this morning."

Maggie sniffed at them. "They smell great."

"Yeah, they're pretty good," Elsie said. "There's

cereal in the cupboard and juice in the refrigerator. You're supposed to be a wife, so I guess you could help yourself." She took a bun and broke it up in a bowl for Horatio. "He's got a sweet tooth," she said to Hank.

"Yeah," Hank said, "and you've got a soft heart."

"Well, don't let it get around," Elsie said. "People take advantage."

A huge bear of a man ambled through the back door. "Howdy," he said. "Smells like cinnamon buns here. Boy, I love cinnamon buns."

Elsie looked at Hank. "He belong to you?"

"Afraid so. This is my best friend, Bubba."

Bubba turned his attention to Maggie. "Wow," he said softly. "I don't mean to stare, but what happened to the rest of your pants?"

Maggie tugged at the cutoff sweats. "I wasn't expecting company."

"I'm not company," Bubba said. "I'm Bubba."

"I'm Maggie," she said, shaking his hand.

Bubba took a cinnamon bun and tore off a huge chunk. "So, why'd you have to go and get married?" he said to Hank. "One day you just disappeared, and we all thought you got run out of town by some husband, or something. Then next thing here you are married." He leaned across the table and lowered his voice. "Is she pregnant?"

"No. I'm not pregnant," Maggie said. "Do you want coffee?"

"Do bears crap in the woods?" Bubba said grinning.

Maggie rolled her eyes and poured the coffee. "I'd like to stay and chat, but I have work to do." She took a roll and her coffee and eased herself out of the kitchen.

"She's pretty," Bubba said, "but I still don't see why you had to marry her."

"She just begged and begged," Hank told him. "It was pitiful."

Maggie paused halfway to the stairs and considered going back into the kitchen to strangle her fake husband. He had a diabolical sense of humor, and he loved provoking her. Strangling would be satisfying, she thought, but it involved touching, and probably it was best to avoid physical contact. Once she got started there was no telling what she might do.

By ten-thirty she was flying through Chapter One. Bubba had left and Hank was working in his orchard with a machine that was going "thunk, thunk, thunk." The day's heat was filtering through the open window as Maggie tapped a sentence into her computer. She paused to study what she'd written.

She supposed most people would frown on what Aunt Kitty had done, but she didn't feel it was her place to judge. Aunt Kitty had lived to be ninety-three years old, and Maggie had known her as an old woman. She'd been kind, intelligent, and in love with life. Her diary had been filled with wonderful trivia, pressed flowers, romantic images, and from time to time the confessions of self-doubt and regret of a woman who'd spent the prime of her life in disrepute.

The bulk of the diary consisted of the day-to-day business of running a bordello, and this is what Maggie found most fascinating: The number of linens purchased, the salary of the piano player, the garters ordered from a specialty shop in New Orleans, the bills from the iceman, coal company, green grocer. Mixed in with all of this were descriptions of customers, hilarious anecdotes, and trade secrets that were for the most part unpublishable.

Two hours later Hank stood in the open door to Maggie's study and watched her work. She looked completely absorbed in her project. She was typing rapidly, occasionally referring to the pad at her elbow, occasionally stopping to read from the screen. She muttered something and gestured with her hand. She shook her head and began typing again.

Desire slid through him. If he hadn't been holding her lunch in his hand, he might have locked the door behind him and taken his chances. As it was, he watched her for a moment more, trying to understand her determination.

He found it hard to take this writing business seriously. Maybe if she'd wanted to write science fiction, or a book for kids . . . but a book about a madam? It seemed more like a hobby or a whim to him. Like looking up your genealogy. And it seemed presumptuous to simply sit down to write a book. He imagined there were skills to be learned, a style to be developed. It probably wasn't much different from growing apple trees, he thought. First you had to acquire a lot of knowledge, and then you had to make a lot of mistakes.

In the meantime she was going to be the scandal of Skogen, and she was going to ruin his last chance to get a loan. He should be furious. But he wasn't. He understood about crazy ideas and substituting enthusiasm for expertise. And he was head over heels in love with her.

He rapped on the doorjamb to get her attention. "I brought you some lunch," he said.

She put her hand to her heart. "You startled me!"

"Mmmm. You look pretty wrapped up in this. How's it going?"

"Great! I've researched and planned this book for two years, and it's practically writing itself. I've had it all in my head, you see—" She bit into the egg salad sandwich. "Probably when I get farther into the book it'll slow down, but it's so satisfying to finally see it on the screen."

"Do I get to read it?"

"When I'm farther along." She wolfed down her sandwich, drank her iced tea, and wiped her mouth. "That was good. Thanks. I didn't realize I was so hungry."

Hank took the plate and the empty glass. "Elsie's going into town. She wants to know if you need anything."

"Nope. I'm fine."

He hated to leave her. He wanted to stay and talk and learn about all the horrible things she did as a kid. He wanted to know if she was ever afraid or lonely or discouraged. He wanted to know about the men in her life and how she felt about babies. He searched for an excuse to prolong lunch.

"Would you like dessert? Elsie made chocolate chip cookies this morning."

"I'm absolutely stuffed. Maybe later."

"Okay, 'bye."

It was six o'clock and Elsie was bustling around the kitchen. "We got chicken soup for supper tonight," she said, slapping plates and bowls onto the kitchen table. "There's corn bread in the oven and chocolate pudding in the refrigerator for dessert."

Hank looked at the two place settings. "Aren't you eating with us? Is there something good on television again?"

"I got a date. I met this nice young man in town today. He don't look a day over sixty-five. We're going to get a burger, and then he said there's a bingo game in Mount Davie."

Hank mentally reviewed all the old men in town. "Is this Ed Garber?"

"Yup. That's him. Said he was the postmaster until he retired, and that his wife had died three years ago."

"Better watch out," Hank said. "I hear he only has one thing on his mind."

"Lord bless him, and he likes to play bingo too. Life don't get much better than that."

Elsie took her apron off and put it in a drawer. "I saw that Linda Sue at the supermarket today. She was checking out groceries, and I tell you she could put a newspaper right out of business. Everywhere I went in town people were talking about you getting married to a dirty book writer. I wouldn't hold my breath for that loan. Your reputation's about as good as snake spit."

"She's not a dirty book writer. She's writing about her Aunt Kitty."

Elsie looked skeptical. "Don't get me wrong. I like Maggie. She's got something to her. And if I were you and had to make a choice, I'd take Maggie over an apple press any day of the year."

Hank smiled at her. "You're a pretty smart lady."

"You'd better believe it, and I'm in good shape for being so old too."

She took her purse from the counter when Ed Garber knocked at the front door.

"You'd better go pull Maggie's nose out of

that computer and get her down here while the corn bread's hot. And it wouldn't hurt to do something with her after supper. It isn't natural for a body to sit that long. All her insides will get cramped up. I once knew someone who sat all day like that and nature never could take its course. Before you know it, you're taking prunes and milk of magnesia when all you ever needed in the first place was to go for a walk once in a while."

Ed Garber looked in at Hank. "Howdy," he said. "Nice day."

"Yup. Good weather for growing apples."

"You still growing them organic? Don't you have more than your share of rot?"

"I have to work at it, but so far they look fine," Hank said.

"I should stop around sometime and see how you do it. I've got an apple tree in my backyard that's plain pitiful."

Hank closed the screen door on Elsie and Ed, and went upstairs after Maggie.

"Elsie says you have to come down to supper while the corn bread's hot," he told her. "And she says your insides will cramp up if you sit here much more. Then nature won't be able to take its course, and you'll have to eat prunes."

Maggie finished typing a sentence and saved her file. "You sound skeptical, but she's probably right."

"I'm supposed to make sure you get exercise."

Maggie shut the computer down. "I could use some exercise. We could go for a walk after supper."

"That was my second choice."

She wasn't going to ask him about choice number one. "Would it hurt the apple trees if we walked through the orchard?"

"Nope. It's crisscrossed with truck paths."

In the kitchen Maggie ladled out the soup and took the corn bread from the oven. They sat across from each other in companionable silence while they ate.

"This is nice," she finally said. "I always hated eating supper alone. Sometimes I'd set the table and fuss with a meal, but most of the time I stuck a frozen burrito in the microwave and ate standing up."

He grinned at her. "Does your mother know that?"

She laughed. "My mother is afraid to ask. And if my mother's neighbor Mrs. Ciak ever found out . . ." Maggie shook her head. "My mother would be disgraced forever." She buttered another piece of corn bread.

"At night, in my parents' neighborhood, no one draws the shades downstairs. It would mean that you didn't want anyone to see in. People would speculate that your house wasn't clean. And all the women have dryers, but they still hang sheets outdoors because if you don't someone might think your sheets weren't white enough to be seen. I know it sounds silly, but it makes me feel claustrophobic. All those unwritten rules. All those comparisons. And as much as I tried, I could never fit my square peg into Riverside's round hole. I guess I was too stubborn."

"I notice you're using that in the past tense."

Maggie chewed her corn bread. "I'm better now." Hank raised his eyebrows and Maggie laughed. "You're right, I'm still stubborn. But being stubborn can be good when you're an adult. Now I like to think of myself as having tenacity, strength of conviction, and character."

Hank pushed away from the table. He went to the refrigerator, took out two puddings, and gave one to Maggie. "Is that why you wanted to come to Vermont? To get away from the white sheets and open windows?"

"I wanted to make a new beginning. I needed to be anonymous."

Hank averted his eyes and dipped his spoon into his pudding. It sounded to him like she'd jumped from the frying pan into the fire. Skogen was the gossip capital of the free world. He was sure every person in town knew what Maggie had worn last night, what she'd eaten, and what she'd said. And they were judging her. Riverside wasn't the only town where sheets were hung out to dry. It wasn't something he wanted to tell her right now. She'd find out soon enough for herself. And if she gave the town half a chance, she'd find out it had some redeeming qualities too.

They cleaned the kitchen and set out for their walk with Horatio trotting close on their heels. There was still plenty of sunlight so Hank headed south, taking a truck path that crossed the longest stretch of his property. It was July and the trees were thick with immature apples.

"What will happen to these apples if you don't get the loan?" Maggie wanted to know. "Will they just rot?"

"No. It's not really that drastic. I belong to a

co-op. I can put them in controlled atmosphere storage, or I can wholesale them."

"Oh." There was a blank look to her face that told him she didn't know much about the apple market.

"There are three ways you can market an apple," he told her. "Direct marketing means that you sell your own product at your doorstep. Regional marketing is selling your product locally, like I do at Big Irma's. And the third alternative is wholesale when you go through an apple broker and sell your apples in bulk. You make the least profit and run the greatest risk when you wholesale. I want to develop my direct and regional marketing. I want to cater to the visiting skiers and the affluent, nutrition-conscious yuppies that migrate here from Boston and New York. I'm not at full production yet. It will take another seven years before all my trees reach maturity, but already I'm producing the apples I need to diversify."

"So you won't go broke if you don't get the loan."

He picked up a stone and skimmed it across the dusty road. "It's not entirely a matter of money. If I have a good crop, I won't go broke, but I won't make any progress either. I don't need to be a millionaire, but I need to have something of my own. Some success that I made happen." He looked over at her to see if she understood.

"I was the kid that almost got an A in school. I almost made it to big-time hockey. I almost graduated from college. It's important to me to see this through to the end. Just once I need to reach the goal I've set for myself. It's not an unrealistic goal. I should be able to achieve it."

"How soon do you need the money?"

He looked at the apples hanging on the trees all around him. "Yesterday would have been good. Last week would have been better." He watched her brows knit together, and he ruffled her hair. They were supposed to be walking to get her intestines uncramped, not to discuss his business.

"Don't pay any attention to me. I'm too impatient. Sooner or later I'll get the loan, and everything will work out. There's always another apple crop. I know exactly what equipment I need. I have the ground set aside and all the utilities are in for a small bottling plant and a bakery."

"Where are you going to build?"

"At the westernmost tip of my property. I could set the buildings back far enough from the road, behind a stand of Paula Reds, so they wouldn't be an eyesore. The ground is level, and there's a good water source."

"How about labor?"

"To work in the bakery? Skogen is stable, but it isn't flourishing. It could use the taxes and jobs I'd generate."

"Hard to believe your father isn't willing to invest in this."

"My father *never* takes chances. He doesn't even own a paisley tie—only stripes in subdued colors. He orders his shoes through a catalog and has worn the same style for thirty-five years. Every morning he has six ounces of orange juice, oatmeal, and a cup of black coffee. He wouldn't consider a strip of bacon or a glass of cran-grape."

"I probably shouldn't have told him about Aunt Kitty."

Hank took her hand and kissed a fingertip. "You were right to tell him. It wouldn't do to start out a marriage with secrets, would it?"

Maggie groaned. She'd groaned partly because it was such a ridiculous thing for him to say, but mostly she'd groaned when his lips touched her skin. She snatched her hand away and stuffed it into the pocket of her shorts for safekeeping. "Were you really the scourge of Skogen?"

"I never thought of myself in exactly those terms, but I suppose I put fear into the hearts of a few mothers."

Maggie had no trouble believing that.

"Physically I was one of those early maturers," he told her with a grin. "Emotional maturity took a little longer. About fifteen years longer."

"So, you think you've finally achieved it, huh?"

"Definitely. Look at me; I'm married and everything."

"I don't mean to burst your bubble, but you're not married. You're pretending to be married. Most people wouldn't consider that to be a sign of mental health. And there is no *everything*. There isn't even *something*."

"You're wrong," he said nudging against her. "There's *something*."

She raised a haughty eyebrow.

His thumb brushed across the nape of her neck. "Go ahead, admit it. There's *something*, isn't there?"

A delicious shiver traveled the length of her spine. "There might be something."

"Damn right," he said, whirling her around, pulling her into the circle of his arms. His hands roamed over her back, pressing her closer, his mouth lowered to hers, and his tongue swept away what little resistance she'd been able to muster. He heard her small gasp of delight, felt her yield to him, and was immediately uncomfortable with the fit of his jeans. It was like being sent back to puberty, he thought. He was out of control. He was in love. And he was hurting. He pushed her away, holding her at arm's length, and took a deep breath. "We could actually get married, you know."

If he'd been serious, she would have been furious. As it was, she attributed his proposal to his awful sense of humor and his forced abstinence.

He pressed his lips together, feeling like a fool. "I can see that took you by surprise."

"I'm getting used to being surprised. Besides, it wasn't such a surprise. It was testosterone talking."

He couldn't deny it. Still, he'd lived with testosterone attacks for a lot of years, and he'd never before asked a woman to marry him. "So, what's the answer?"

Maggie rolled her eyes.

"I suppose that's a no."

"Are you relieved?"

A small smile curved at the corners of his mouth. "Maybe a little." He slid his hands down to her hips. "But not entirely. I like having you in my house."

Maggie backed away. Smooth, she thought. He had good moves. Moves that were undoubtedly designed to throw her off guard. Disarming one minute, and then charming the next. He was clever all right, but she was cleverer. She didn't trust him for a second.

"I think you're just trying to get out of walking," she said. "I think you're lazy."

The grin widened. "No, you don't. You think I'm only out for one thing, and I'm sweet-talking you."

She felt the flush creep into her cheeks. "Well, you are the scourge of Skogen."

"True. But I've changed. All that's behind me. It's been years since I've been worth anything as a scourge."

"What about Linda Sue and Holly?"

Linda Sue and Holly felt like part of his

extended family. He'd grown up with them. They made girlfriend noises, but it had been a long time since he'd found them exciting. Not since high school, in fact. And anything in a skirt had been exciting when he was in high school. "Linda Sue and Holly are my friends."

"Have you explained that to them lately?"

"Linda Sue and Holly are good at talking, short on listening."

Chapter 5

"Tell me about apples," Maggie said, following the rutted road. "I want to know about your orchard."

"I grow five varieties of apples. The original orchard was all McIntosh, but I've put in Paula Reds, Empire, Red Delicious, and Northern Spy. It's extended my growing season, and I think the blend of apples makes a more interesting cider." He picked a small green apple. "This is a Northern Spy. It's the apple I intend to build my pie business around. It's a hard baking apple. Matures late in the season. Keeps well." He threw the apple down the road and Horatio took off after it.

So, he had to prove himself, she thought. She could relate to that. Her life wasn't exactly filled with stellar accomplishments. She'd barely graduated from college, barely hung on to her teaching job, barely kept her sanity in Riverside. She was one of those women who put their sheets in the dryer because she knew damn well they wouldn't measure up.

It was kind of funny that she and Hank had come together. Two misfits aiming for their first real success. And how were they doing it? He wanted to bake pies, and she was writing about a madam. They were outrageous.

They walked until they came to a stream. "Goose Creek," Hank said. "My land ends here. When I was a kid, I spent a lot of time fishing and swimming in Goose Creek. If you follow it downstream, it fans out into a nice deep pool."

Maggie stood on the grassy bank and stared at the water. The colors of the land were muted, the sky was brilliant with a sunset, and Goose Creek gurgled as it rushed over rocks. She thought this would be a nice place to be a little boy. Goose Creek and cows and row after row of apple trees. It was the American Dream.

When Aunt Kitty was a little girl there had been farms like this surrounding Riverside. Now there were shopping malls and highways and houses. Lots and lots of houses. And lots and lots of people. The people spilled out of the houses, clogging the roads and the supermarket aisles. Maggie'd had to stand in line to go to a movie, cash a check, buy a loaf of bread. And now here she was—just her and Hank and Goose Creek. It felt a little odd. All she could hear was Goose Creek and a cow, mooing in the distance. A cow, for crying out loud. Who would believe it.

"I think I'm experiencing culture shock," she told Hank.

"What's the matter, don't they have cows in Riverside?" He moved closer, draping an arm around her shoulders. He felt her stiffen and gave her shoulder a gentle squeeze. "Don't worry. This is a friendly gesture. I've decided not to put any big moves on you until your opinion of me changes."

"Gee, thanks."

"I'm not even going to repeat my proposal of marriage for a while. I mean, after all, who would want to marry the scourge of Skogen?"

She could hear a hint of laughter in his voice. It pulled at her, causing her to shake her head and smile with him. He was a man who could laugh at himself. That was nice. She suspected he was also a man who knew how to manipulate a situation. So she was still going to be careful. "Seems to me there are a number of women in town who would be more than happy to marry you."

"Yeah," he said, "but they only want me for my apples."

Before they returned to the house, total blackness had descended on the orchard. Without benefit of a moon, they slowly, blindly picked their way along the dirt road.

"You sure you know where you're going?" Maggie asked.

"Of course I know where I'm going. This is my apple orchard."

"There aren't any bears around here, are there?"

"The closest thing we have to a bear is Bubba, and he's pretty much harmless. Of course, if you're afraid you can come cuddle up to me, and I'll protect you."

"I thought you weren't making any more moves."

"If I'm not breathing heavy, it doesn't count as a move." He groped for her hand in the darkness. "Give me your hand, and I'll make sure you get home safe and sound."

She slid her hand into his, not because she was afraid, but because, even though his reputation left something to be desired, she liked him enormously. He was fun and he was comfortable. And she liked the way her hand felt in his. It felt like it belonged there. She was feeling a little homesick for all of the things she used to hate about Riverside, and it was good to know that at least her hand was in the right place.

They crested a small hill and were greeted by a single dot of light. Elsie had put the porch light on before she'd gone off on her date. Hank guided Maggie to the front porch and opened the screen door.

"We forgot to lock up the house," Maggie said. "We didn't even close the door."

"I can't remember the last time I locked this house. I don't even know if I have a key."

"My Lord, anyone could walk right in."

"I guess that's true, but no one ever has. Except Bubba, of course. And Bubba wouldn't care if the door was locked. He'd just give it a good kick and that would be the end of that."

"Don't you have any crime in Skogen?"

He switched the light on in the foyer. "Not since I promised to behave myself. And that was a good while ago." He went into the kitchen and looked into the refrigerator. "I could use a pudding. How about you?"

Maggie got two spoons from the silverware drawer. "A pudding sounds great." She sat across from him at the table and dug into her pudding. "What sort of crimes did you commit before going straight?"

"The usual teenage stuff. I borrowed a couple cars."

"Borrowed?"

"Technically I guess I stole them. But they were my father's. And I always returned them with a full tank of gas."

"Anything else?"

"Got a few speeding tickets. Got caught buying beer with a forged ID a couple times."

"I know you're saving something good for last."

"There was this thing about Bucky Weaver's barn, but it really wasn't my fault."

Maggie cocked an eyebrow. "Am I going to need another pudding to see me through this?"

"Wouldn't hurt."

She took the last two puddings out of the refrigerator and gave one to Hank.

"It was a deciding factor in whether or not I should try pro hockey," he said. "Actually I had my choice of hockey or the army."

"Uh-huh."

A splash of color appeared on his cheeks. He really wasn't enjoying this, but he wanted to tell her before she heard it somewhere else. His whole childhood had been a struggle for independence. In fact, looking back, he thought his childhood had been a struggle for survival. There'd been no room in his father's rigid lifestyle for a little boy with chocolate on his face. His father had no patience with a seven-year-old who couldn't color inside the lines, or a fourteen-year-old who couldn't tie a perfect Windsor knot, or a seventeen-year-old who was put into remedial reading because it was finally discovered he had dyslexia.

Every time Hank failed by his father's standards, the rules and restrictions grew tighter. And the more rules his father imposed, the more Hank had rebelled. If he wasn't going to get approval, then he sure as hell was going to get attention.

After a couple of years on his own knocking around the hockey circuit he'd grown up, thank heaven. Now he set his own moral standards and imposed his own rules of conduct. The only approval he needed was his own. Until Maggie. Falling in love, he discovered, brought with it a whole new set of needs and responsibilities.

He looked at Maggie sitting across from him and took a deep breath. "One night, about a week before graduation, I persuaded Bucky's daughter, Jenny, to meet me in the barn behind her house. We had a six-pack of beer. We were up in the loft and it was dark, so I lit the kerosene lantern. Bucky saw the light go on and thought he had a thief in his barn. I don't know what he thought the thief was stealing, because the barn was empty except for about twelve years' worth of pigeon droppings. Anyway, he got his old bear gun down from the mantel and blasted the hell out of his barn."

"Was anyone hurt?"

Hank grinned. "No. But he hit the lantern and burned his barn down."

Maggie clamped her hand over her mouth to keep from laughing out loud. "It must have been terrible," she finally managed.

He was relieved she could see the humor in it. It hadn't been too funny at the time, and years later, when he'd returned to Skogen, people were still telling the story about the time Bucky Weaver burned his barn down. "It was a turning point in my life," he told her. "I had to leave Skogen, and it was the best thing that ever happened to me."

"But you came back."

He shrugged. "It's home."

Maggie wasn't sure she felt the same way about Riverside. She'd been born and raised there, and she felt a flurry of homesickness from time to time, but she wasn't sure it was home.

"Couldn't home be somewhere else? Isn't there any place else you'd like to live?"

He stared at the four empty pudding dishes on the table. He hadn't really given it much thought. At least not in a long time. Home had always been his granny's house, even when he was a kid. This was where he'd laughed and played and felt safe. After his granny had died and he'd moved into her house, he'd realized it wasn't the house that had made it a home. It had been his granny. Now Maggie made it a home. Home was with Maggie, and he supposed it could be anywhere in the world. He found it astonishing that he could feel that way about a woman he'd known less than a week.

"I guess one place would be as good as another," he told her, "but it's hard to move a hundred and ten acres of apple trees. They don't pack well."

* * *

It was dark in Maggie's room. The window was open, but there was no breeze to stir the curtains, no moon to splash silvery light across her floor. She'd come awake fast with her heart pounding in her chest, her throat tight with fear. She was afraid to open her eyes. Afraid to move. Afraid the intruder would notice her altered breathing pattern. She tried to think, but her mind was a blind alley that had no outlet for her panic.

Someone was in her room. She could feel it. She *knew* he was there. Clothing rustled. A board creaked in the floor. Her eyes flew open in time to see a shadow move toward the door. It was a man, and her first thought was of Hank. Let it be Hank, she prayed.

The shadow hurried into the dark hall and Maggie heard Horatio growl. The sound came from deep in the dog's throat, low and threatening. He was moving slowly and stealthily across the floor, stalking the man. Maggie felt as if the house were holding its breath, and then all hell broke loose as Horatio bolted out of the bedroom. The intruder thundered down the stairs; his only concern to escape from the dog.

Maggie was out of bed. She ran into the hall and saw Hank disappear down the stairwell after Horatio. A bloodcurdling scream carried from the front lawn, and then there was the sound of a car door slamming and a car being gunned down the driveway.

Maggie met Hank in the foyer. She reached out for him with a shaking hand, and found nothing but warm skin to hang on to. He'd only taken the time to pull on a pair of jeans. She flattened against him in her cotton nightshirt, and, to her own disgust, began to cry.

"He was in my room! I woke up, and he was moving around in my room! I don't know what he was doing, or how long he'd been in there—"

She was babbling, but she couldn't help it. It was the first time in her life she'd ever felt truly frightened. The first time she'd felt endangered and helpless.

Now that it was over, she was shaking from the inside out. She clamped her teeth together to keep them from chattering and pressed her forehead against Hank's chest. She was hysterical, she thought . . . and she hated it. She stiffened her spine, pulled away from him, and took several deep breaths.

"Okay," she said. "I'm better now." She wiped her eyes with the back of her hand. "You must think I'm an idiot, bursting into tears like some wimp."

Hank eased her back to him. "If I'd known you'd turn to me in terror like that, I'd have hired someone to break into your room last night."

He kissed her hair and smoothed his hands along the curve of her spine, feeling her warmth creep through the thin cotton. His arms wrapped around her, bringing her closer until she was snug against him. He'd given her a glib answer, but he didn't feel so casual inside. He was furious that someone had violated his house, and he was horrified that the intruder had been in Maggie's room.

Maggie splayed her hand flat to his chest. "Your heart is racing."

"It's your nightie."

She gave him a playful slap, but he held tight. "I'm not ready to let go yet," he told her. "If you want to know the truth, I'm probably more scared than you are. The thought of some *slime*bug crawling around in your room has my stomach churning."

He buried his face in her hair and swore to

himself that this wouldn't happen again. As soon as the sun came up, he'd install locks on the doors, and from now on Horatio would sleep with Maggie.

Elsie came grumbling into the foyer. She was wearing big blue fuzzy slippers and a long blue housecoat, and her short, steel-gray hair was standing on end in crazy, electrified-looking tufts.

"What the devil's going on out here? Sounded like someone was dropping bowling balls down the stairs. Men screaming outside, dogs barking. I'm an old lady. I need my sleep."

"Someone broke into the house," Maggie said. "He was sneaking around in my room, and then Horatio chased him down the stairs."

Elsie's mouth dropped open. "If that don't beat all." Her eyes narrowed and her lips thinned in a tight smile. "Well, I'd like to see him try that again. I'll be waiting for him from now on. I know how to protect myself, you know."

"Where's Horatio?" Maggie asked. "Is he okay?"

Hank looked out the open front door. "Last I saw him he was chasing the car down the driveway."

Hank gave a sharp whistle through his teeth, and Horatio came loping onto the porch. He trotted inside and dropped a piece of denim at Hank's feet.

Elsie stooped to get the ragged material. "Hmmph," she said, "it's from the cuff. If I were a dog, I would have sunk my teeth in a mite higher." She gave the scrap back to Horatio and patted him on the head. "Good dog. You aren't exactly a killer, but you did good anyway."

She turned around in her big blue slippers and shuffled off to her room. "I'm going back to bed. Let me know if there's any more excitement."

Hank closed the front door and scowled at the lock. It was old and he didn't have a key. He was afraid if he ever did manage to get it locked, he might never be able to get it unlocked.

"I'll get this fixed as soon as the hardware store opens," he told Maggie. "Do you have any idea what this guy was doing in your room?"

She shook her head. "By the time I saw him, he was heading for the door."

Hank looked at the pendulum wall clock in the foyer. "It's three-thirty. Why don't you go to bed, and I'll look around down here to see if anything's been stolen."

"I'll check the rooms upstairs."

Half an hour later they sat side by side on the edge of Maggie's bed and concluded nothing had been taken. The only room to seem disrupted had been Maggie's bedroom. The intruder had gone through her dresser drawers, and he hadn't been too neat about it.

"I can't figure it," Hank said. "You had almost fifty dollars in small bills laying on your dresser top. And he left it. He didn't take your pearl earrings or watch. What the devil was he looking for?"

A silly idea skittered through Maggie's mind. Ridiculous, she thought. I'm getting paranoid. But when she looked at Hank, she knew he'd had the same thought. "You don't suppose he was looking for this?" She opened her night drawer and pulled out Aunt Kitty's diary.

"Hard to believe. I'm sure everyone thinks it's got a lot of hot stuff in it, but I can't imagine someone breaking and entering just to get their hands on a dirty book."

Maggie gave him a look.

"Okay, okay," he said. "So, it crossed my mind too, but you have to admit it doesn't make any sense. This isn't the Hope diamond we're talking about here. This is an old lady's diary. I know everyone in Skogen. I can't come up with anyone who would want that diary enough to steal it."

"Everybody too honest?"

"No. All the likely candidates are too lazy."

"Maybe it's not someone in Skogen," Maggie said. "Maybe word has spread throughout the state, throughout the country."

"Maybe someone followed you up here from New Jersey. This could be serious," Hank said, flopping back onto the bed. "I'd better sleep here tonight and make sure you're safe."

"You never give up, do you?"

"This is an emergency situation."

She looked at him sprawled across her bed and swallowed. He was magnificent. Smooth, tanned skin, a hard, flat stomach, and jeans that were zipped but not snapped.

Good thing she wasn't one of those women who lost control at the sight of perfect flesh and muscle, she thought. Actually she had to admit her control was slipping a little. There was a certain appeal to spending the rest of the night with him, and it had nothing to do with safety. It had to do with the lovely flush of desire his presence generated. The need to touch him was almost overwhelming. If she'd been more experienced, she might have given in to it. But as it was, she regarded it curiously and with a little awe.

She'd never felt such a compelling, delicious ache to know a man. Never *needed* to be loved. She wondered if he had similar feelings, and then she realized with a shock that of course he did . . . he was the sex fiend of Skogen. He probably felt that way about every woman he met.

Disappointment hit her like a hard slap in the face. She narrowed her eyes. "I'm giving you thirty seconds to get off my bed. I don't sleep with indiscriminate womanizers."

She saw the expression of playful affection change to one of hurt and surprise, then anger. Direct hit, she thought grimly.

Hank heaved himself to his feet. He thought she understood the man behind the reputation. Hank whistled for Horatio. The dog trotted into Maggie's room and looked at his master expectantly. "Stay," Hank told him, and without even so much as a backward glance at Maggie, he strode from the room and slammed the door behind him.

He'd been honest with her. Hank fumed. What more did she want? He turned on his heel and went back to Maggie's room, yanking the door open. "You have a lot of nerve calling me an indiscriminate womanizer. I've been beyond reproach since you've been here."

"I've been here for three days!" Maggie shouted. "You expect me to be impressed with three days of abstinence? And for all I know you've been sneaking out at night, burning down barns."

He felt the heat flooding into his face again. He stormed into his own room and slammed his door.

Maggie sprang up from her bed. "And don't come barging into my room without knocking!" she shouted. Then she slammed her door too.

She threw herself into bed and pulled the quilt up to her chin. She grunted and rolled over, stuffing her face into the pillow. "Men!" she said. "Ugh!" She thrashed around for a few more minutes until her bedclothes were totally tangled. She got up, remade the bed, and calmly crawled back in. She was hot and exhausted and sorry. She shouldn't have made that crack about the barn burning.

"Damn stubborn temper," she said. A tear rolled down her cheek. She wanted Hank to love her. Only her. She didn't want to be just one more conquest, one more event. She wanted to be special, and she didn't want to suffer the fate of his other girlfriends. She didn't want to turn into a Hank Mallone groupie.

Elsie slammed bowls of oatmeal onto the table. "Anyone who doesn't eat this and like it gets liver for supper."

Hank rattled his paper, and Maggie tapped a spoon against her coffee mug.

"And I don't put up with spoon tapping neither," Elsie said. "I feel darn cranky. I didn't get any sleep last night. Bad enough we got some fool wandering around the upstairs, then the two of you decide to have a shouting match and door-slamming contest. I got more rest when I was living in the old people's home. The most noise anybody made was when they dropped their bedpan. Except for the time Helen Grote set her walker down on the cat's tail."

The memory brought a smile to her face. "That was something."

Hank folded his paper and placed it on the table beside his oatmeal. He glared briefly at Maggie and splashed milk onto his bowl.

Maggie glared back. Fine. If he wanted to be childish and stay angry, so would she. No problem for her, she thought. She could stay angry forever. After all, she was the most stubborn female Riverside had ever spawned. She could show him a thing or two.

The trouble was she didn't want to stay angry. She wanted to cuddle up behind him while he was eating his oatmeal, wrap her arms around his neck, and kiss him on the top of his head. His hair was freshly washed and shiny and looked like it would be nice to kiss. His cheek looked like it would be nice to kiss too. And his mouth . . . Maggie sighed at the thought of kissing his mouth.

The sigh prompted him to glance up from his oatmeal. He stared at her, but he didn't say anything. He looked annoyed.

"Well, excuse me," she snapped. "Did my sigh disturb you?"

"Don't flatter yourself. It would take a lot more than a sigh to get me to notice you."

Elsie made a disgusted sound and plunked a platter of French toast on the table. "What are you two so bent out of shape about? This is the most realistic fake marriage I've ever seen. If you get any more married, you'll have to get a divorce."

The back door opened and Bubba ambled in. "I knew I smelled French toast."

Elsie stood with her hand on her hip. "How many loaves do you eat?"

"One will be fine," Bubba said. "Don't go to any bother."

Elsie took more eggs out of the refrigerator. "Don't you have a home?" she asked. "Why aren't you married?"

"I'm not the marrying type," Bubba said. "Besides, it wouldn't be right for me to tie myself down to one woman. It wouldn't be fair to all those other females out there that crave my attention."

Maggie hid behind her half of the newspaper and made a gagging gesture.

"It's especially critical that I keep my bachelor status now that Hank's no longer in circulation," Bubba said. "Someone's gotta take up the slack." He shook his head. "All those heartbroken women . . ." He sighed and poured syrup on four slices of French toast. "I'm just about exhausted with it."

Hank grinned. "Bubba's been going with the

same girl since high school. If Bubba so much as looked at anyone else, she'd nail his shoes to the floor and turn him into a gelding with a bread knife."

"Oh man," Bubba said, "you're always ruining my image."

Maggie thought Bubba was the human counterpart to Brer Bear. And he was probably almost as smart as Brer Bear, she decided. She reprimanded herself for being snide, but she couldn't help it. She was in a foul mood this morning.

Bubba forked toast into his mouth. "This sure is good," he said. "I might think about getting married if I could find a woman who could cook like this." He gave Elsie a questioning look.

"Forget it," Elsie said. "I'm too old for you, and besides, if I wasn't getting paid, I'd be eating TV dinners."

"Too bad," Bubba said. "Peggy keeps wanting me to go on a diet. For breakfast she fixes me half a cup of those little high-fiber nugget things in some skim milk. It's like scarfing down buckshot in water."

"Maybe you could stand to lose a few pounds," Elsie offered, as she watched him wolf down the French toast.

Bubba glanced at his stomach. "It's cause I sit on a loader all day. I don't get enough exercise."

"Bubba has a backhoe and a front-end loader," Hank explained. "He does construction jobs. He's working on the site for my bottling plant this week."

Bubba took a sip of coffee. "So, how's the book going?" he said to Maggie. "I was talking to Elmo Feeley at the feed store, and he said the book is full of sex, and you've already been asked to make it into a movie."

Maggie's fork slithered through her fingers and clattered onto her plate. Her mouth hung open, but she couldn't find her voice. Even if she'd had a voice, she wouldn't have known what to say.

Hank set his coffee cup down and looked from Maggie to Bubba. It was the first time he'd seen Maggie tongue-tied and he rather liked it. She'd been quick to believe the worst about him, he thought. Now he was interested to see how she handled a little false notoriety about herself.

"Yup," Hank said, smiling at Bubba, "Cupcake here is going to be rich." He leaned closer to Bubba and dropped his voice to a whisper.

117

"That's why I married her, you know. I needed money for the cider press and the bakery equipment."

Maggie sucked in her breath and narrowed her eyes. He was doing it again!

"And is the book really full of sex?" Bubba asked.

"You wouldn't believe what's in that diary," Hank said. "Maggie and I have been going through it, page by page, for the last three nights, and it's got stuff in there I've never even thought of. We've been trying it all out just to make sure a person can really do it. Maggie wouldn't put anything in her book that she hasn't personally experienced. You know, sort of like testing recipes before you write a cookbook."

Bubba chuckled and punched Hank in the arm. "You dog, you."

Elsie hit Hank on the head with her wooden spoon. "The Lord's gonna get you for that." She bit her lip to keep from laughing out loud and quickly turned back to the stove.

Maggie's mouth was still open, and she'd taken hold of the table. Her knuckles were turning white and her eyes were small and glittery.

"Maybe you should go easy on the diary stuff for a while," Bubba whispered to Hank. "She looks a little on edge, you know what I mean?"

"It's the way she gets," Hank said. "Hungry. All you have to do is mention the diary, and she turns into an animal. She's just trying to control herself. That's why she's holding on to the table. She doesn't want to rip my clothes off at the breakfast table."

"Wow," Bubba said. "Are you doing okay? I mean, she isn't hurting you or anything, is she?"

Hank finished his coffee and winked at Bubba. "I can handle her."

Bubba chuckled and punched him in the arm again.

Hank pushed away from the table. He kissed Maggie on the top of the head and gave her shoulders a squeeze. "I know you're feeling desperate, but I have to go to work now, pumpkin. Maybe you can find some techniques for when I come home at lunch."

"I—you—" she said. She grabbed a jar of strawberry preserves and threw it at the door, but Hank and Bubba had already disappeared down the back stoop. The jar ripped through the screen and smashed against a stack of empty wooden apple crates.

"Did you hear something crash?" Bubba said.

"Don't worry about it," Hank told him. "Sometimes she gets violent when I leave her."

"Crazy about you, huh?"

Chapter 6

Maggie and Elsie stood staring at the hole in the screen door.

"You didn't miss him by much," Elsie said. "It was the screen that slowed you down."

"I didn't really want to hit him. I just wanted to throw something."

Elsie nodded. "Good job."

Maggie grinned. "He would have been disappointed if I hadn't thrown something. He likes to provoke me."

"You mean you weren't really mad?"

"Of course I was mad. He makes me crazy."

Elsie shook her head. "This is too complicated for me. I'm going to do the dishes."

Maggie cleaned the back porch and went upstairs to work. It was going to be another perfect day, she thought. Blue sky and warm with just the tiniest of breezes. In the distance she could hear an engine turn over and guessed it was Bubba on the loader.

She reread the handwritten notes she'd been compiling. The diary lay to her right. It was open to December 3, 1923. Aunt Kitty had talked of the weather, the tragedy of the Thorley baby's death from the croup, and Johnny McGregor, whom she declared to be the handsomest man she'd ever seen. The "diary" actually consisted of seven diaries, covering a span of thirty-two years. Among other things it was a chronicle of love for John McGregor.

Maggie had chosen to treat her book as historical fiction. It would enable her to give a true recording of history, according to Aunt Kitty's wishes, and still ensure her family a measure of privacy.

The thought that someone might have broken into Hank's house to steal the diary sent a chill through her. It would have to be someone sick, because Aunt Kitty wasn't a famous person. The diary wasn't worth much money. It probably wasn't worth *any* money. For that matter, Maggie suspected the book she was writing wouldn't be worth much money either. Her goal was simply to get Aunt Kitty's story in print. That in itself seemed a formidable task.

Twelve hours later Hank leaned against the kitchen counter, drinking milk and eating oatmeal cookies. "She's still up there."

Elsie shook her head. "I tell you she's a woman possessed. Couldn't even coax her down with my meat loaf."

"Maybe I should throw the circuit breaker."

"Maybe you should take out more health insurance first."

"Okay, so I won't throw the circuit breaker. I'll try charming her out of the room." He went to the refrigerator and took out a bottle of Chablis. "A little wine wouldn't hurt either."

The door to her study was closed. He knocked twice and received a muffled answer. He pushed the door open and found Maggie with her arms crossed on the desktop and her face buried in her arms. She was crying her eyes out, making loud sobbing noises. Her shoulders were shaking, and she had tissues clutched in her hands. He rushed to her and put his hand at the nape of her neck. "Maggie, what's wrong?"

She picked her head up and blinked at him. Her face was flushed and tears tracked down her cheeks. "It's so aw-w-wful," she sobbed. Her breath caught in a series of hiccups.

Hank pulled her out of her chair, sat down, and took her onto his lap, cuddling her close. He stroked the hair back from her face and waited while she blew her nose. He thought his heart would break. He had no idea she'd been so miserable.

"Tell me about it, honey. What's so awful?"

"J-J-Johnny McGregor. She loved him terribly. It was b-b-beautiful. But he couldn't marry her."

"She?"

"Aunt Kitty. He couldn't marry her. He had an invalid wife and a little girl."

"Let me get this straight. You're crying your head off because Johnny McGregor couldn't marry Aunt Kitty?"

"It's all in chapter two. I just finished it. It's w-w-wonderful." She wiped the tears from her eyes and took a big gulp of air.

"They were sweethearts, but their parents were against their marrying. Aunt Kitty's father sent her to Boston to live with relatives, and while she was there Aunt Kitty discovered she was pregnant. By then his parents thought she was a tramp. Johnny and Aunt Kitty wrote letters to each other, but neither of them ever received them. Aunt Kitty had her baby in

Boston, thinking Johnny had abandoned her. And after two years of not hearing anything from Aunt Kitty, Johnny married his third cousin Marjorie."

Hank thought if he lived to be a hundred he'd never understand women.

"When Aunt Kitty's father died from a heart attack, she came back home for the funeral, and met Johnny on the street, downtown. It was just as if they'd never been separated. They still loved each other, but now Johnny was married, and his wife was frail, and he had an infant daughter."

"He should have waited for Kitty," Hank said. "He should have gone looking for her. I think this McGregor guy sounds like a jerk."

Maggie smiled between snuffles. Hank was more of a fighter than Johnny McGregor. Hank wouldn't have knuckled under to his parents. And Hank wouldn't have stood still while his sweetheart's father spirited her away.

"So, where did all this take place? Was this in Riverside?"

"No. Aunt Kitty and Johnny lived in Easton, Pennsylvania. Aunt Kitty stayed there so she could be near Johnny, and after some hard times she was befriended by a woman who ran a brothel. One thing led to another, and eventually Aunt Kitty took over as madam. She moved to Riverside when she was an old woman."

"And you've got all this in your book, huh?"

"I will eventually." She gave one last sad sigh and got off his lap. "Chapter two is an emotional chapter."

"I can see that." He half-filled a wineglass with the chilled Chablis and passed it to her.

Maggie took the wine and held it a moment before drinking. She watched while he poured some for himself, and smiled when he clinked glasses in a toast.

"To Aunt Kitty," he said. He took a sip, set the glass on the desk, and reached for the fragile leather-bound book Maggie had left lying open. "Do you mind if I read this?"

"I don't think Aunt Kitty would mind. It's the first volume. She started keeping the diary when she was sixteen."

He read the first page and drank a little more wine. Then he thumbed through the book, reading pages at random. "This is actually very interesting."

"You sound surprised."

"I've always thought girls' diaries were sappy. I always figured it was something you filled with lies and exaggerations and then left laying around for your friends to read."

"I think the middle diaries are the most interesting. They detail household accounts for the brothel. It's a unique slant on history."

Hank selected one of the middle diaries and began reading. His eyes opened wide, and his mouth creased into a broad grin. "Whoa! You were right. This is definitely more interesting. Aunt Kitty had a real flare for words."

"What page are you on?"

"Page forty-two. She's talking about Eugenia and the button salesman."

"Give me that book!"

Hank edged away from her, holding the book too high for her to reach. "Each month Eugenia waited for the button salesman to come into town," Hank read. "Eugenia would wear her sheer red dress and her fancy red-and-black garters . . ."

Maggie lunged for the book, and Hank pinned her against the wall. His eyes were dancing with mischief. "Do you have any garters, Maggie?"

"You're squashing me!"

"Stop squirming. No, on second thought, I think I like the squirming."

She instantly went still. "I'm going to scream for Elsie."

"Coward."

"You bet."

Hank continued to read out loud. "And Eugenia would dot her very best, most expensive French perfume at every pulse point. On the column of her neck . . ." Hank dipped his head and leisurely, thoroughly kissed the pulse point in Maggie's neck. "At her wrist . . ." Hank's mouth moved over Maggie's wrist with slow passion. "Along the heated crevice between her full breasts . . ."

The air felt trapped in Maggie's lungs. Her chest burned with it. Her head hummed with Hank's words, with the sound of his voice, soft and resonant. Desire was rising from somewhere deep inside her and radiating outward in waves that left her weak-kneed.

He'd opened the top buttons on her cotton shirt. It was an outrageous liberty, she thought, but she was powerless to stop him. She wanted to feel his mouth on her breast, and when his lips finally grazed along the soft flesh that swelled from the cup of her lacy bra, she shuddered.

"Should I continue?" he asked.

"Yes." She could barely say it, barely hear her own words over the pounding of her heart.

"She perfumed the tips of her breasts . . ." he said, improvising wildly.

His large hand covered her, molding her to fit his palm. She was soft and full, and he thought he would burst with love. And if he didn't burst from love, he certainly was ready to burst with passion.

He'd thought ahead, and he knew there was only one place left for Eugenia to put the damn perfume. If Maggie allowed him to put his hand there, it was all over.

Then he thought of Elsie, puttering around downstairs in the kitchen and wondered why he'd ever started this.

Maggie had also thought ahead. "Stop," she whispered. "Stop now."

He sagged against her. "You ever seen a grown man cry?"

Maggie giggled from nervousness. "It's not that bad."

"Easy for you to say."

"We have to talk."

"Uh-huh."

She splayed both hands on his chest to put

129

some room between them, but he wouldn't move far.

"I'm going to be honest with you. I'm very attracted to you. It wouldn't take much for me to fall in love and do something foolish, like go to bed with you."

"Why would that be foolish?"

"I'm not like you. Falling in love would be serious for me. It would be painful. It would be disruptive."

A crease formed between his eyebrows. "What makes you think it wouldn't be for me?"

"I think your outlook on life is different from mine."

He held her by the shoulders and gave her a small shake. "You don't know anything about my outlook on life. You don't know anything about me. You only know the stories. Give me a chance, Maggie. Look for yourself."

"I don't want to give you a chance. We have six more months of cohabitation. I don't want to make that any more awkward than it already is. Even if you were the right person for me, this wouldn't work out. Skogen is another Riverside. I'm the prime topic of conversation for the entire town. I'm crazy Maggie Toone all over again, and there probably isn't a man, woman, or child within a fifty-mile radius who isn't waiting to hear about my latest outrageous act."

"You're wrong. You're not crazy Maggie Toone. You're crazy Maggie Mallone."

"I don't want to fall in love with you."

"Fine. Do whatever you can to try to prevent it, but I don't think it will help."

He released her and took a step back. "And what about me? It's too late for me, Maggie. I'm already in love with you."

Disbelief quickly replaced the initial surge of joy. "I suppose that's your problem."

"Wrong. It's *your* problem, because I intend to do whatever is necessary to get you to love me."

"Wasn't it just last night you told me you weren't going to put any moves on me?"

"I changed my mind."

"What made you change your mind?"

"I don't know. I started out wanting to comfort you when you were crying, and I ended up trying to seduce you. About halfway through, it became obvious that I wasn't going to be able to hide my . . . feelings."

Maggie smiled. "You have a point. Your feelings were pretty obvious."

"And you're wrong about Skogen. It's a nice place to live. I think you need to get to know some of the people here. They aren't so bad. They like to gossip, but there isn't anything mean in it. It's just recreation. We don't have a movie theater or a shopping mall, so folks around here spend their time passing along false information."

"I don't know if I want to meet any more Skogenians."

She knew she didn't have a good attitude. After all, she had an obligation to fulfill as his wife.

"Okay, I take that back. I want to meet the locals. What did you have in mind? I hope it's not another dinner party."

"There's a dance at the grange Friday night." Did he just say that? He hated dances.

"A dance?" Her face brightened. "I love dances. What kind of a dance is it?"

Damned if he knew. He'd never been to one. "It's just your average dance, I guess. Elmo Feeley and Andy Snell and some others have a band."

"A live band? And the dance floor, is it wood?"

"It might be."

* * *

Hours later Maggie lay wide-eyed in bed, unable to sleep. She was in love, of course. And of course she'd never admit it to Hank because falling in love with Hank Mallone was a no-win situation.

Still, it was exciting. It was also terrifying. Not terrifying in a daredevil sort of way. That kind of danger had never bothered her. This was real terror. The kind she carried around in the pit of her stomach. The kind that gnawed at her during quiet moments when her mind was unoccupied. Hank Mallone was capable of breaking her heart, and that was much more dangerous than writing a dirty word on a grade school door.

There were slippered footsteps in the hall, and Maggie heard her doorknob turn very slowly, very carefully. There was no light in her room and no light in the hall. Nothing was visible in the dark when the door opened, but Maggie sensed it was Elsie. She was the only one who wore slippers.

"Don't move," Elsie whispered. "And don't say anything. There's a man climbing a ladder up to your window."

"What?"

133

"Shhhh! I said to keep quiet. I'm gonna fix this guy's wagon. When I get done with him, he isn't gonna be climbing ladders for a long time."

That was when Maggie saw the barrel of the gun glint in the blackness. Elsie was right beside her, and she was holding a gun with two hands the way Maggie had seen on the cop shows. "Don't worry about a thing," Elsie said. "I've done this before. I know just where to aim."

A black shape appeared in the far window. A knife sliced along the perimeter of the window screen, and Maggie was able to see that it was a man, and that he was wearing something over his face. A stocking maybe. She and Elsie were hidden in the shadows of the room, but the intruder was slightly backlit from a sliver of moon. He leaned forward to enter the room, and Elsie pulled the trigger.

Maggie thought it had to be like standing next to a howitzer. The blast was deafening, there was a flash of fire from the gun barrel, the smell of smoke and gun oil stung her nostrils, and the man at the window screamed in fright and instantly disappeared. There was a solid thunk as his body hit the ground, followed by the clatter of the ladder falling on top of him.

"Dang, I got excited and shot too soon," Elsie said. "He wasn't even halfway through the window. I probably only shot him in the heart."

Hank rushed into the room, zipping his jeans. "What the devil was that?"

"Elsie shot some guy on a ladder," Maggie said. "He was trying to get into my room."

Hank went to the window and looked through the slashed screen. "I don't think he's shot too bad. I can see him taking off through the orchard. In fact, I don't think he's shot at all since there's a hole the size of a grapefruit in the wall here. How many shots did you fire, Elsie?"

"Just one. He didn't hang around long enough for me to squeeze off another."

"Anybody get a decent look at him?"

"The big sissy was wearing panty hose on his head," Elsie said. "I couldn't hardly see him."

"I didn't see him very well either," Maggie said. "But he seemed bigger than the last man. I think this was someone different. And his scream was different."

"I heard him sneaking around the house," Elsie said. "By the time I got to a window, he was already on the ladder. So I grabbed Little Leroy here and headed for Maggie's room."

Hank gently removed the gun from Elsie's hand and emptied the bullets. "Little Leroy?"

"When I was living in Washington, I bought it at a yard sale. The man who sold me the gun said he called it Little Leroy because it was big and bad just like this friend of his named Leroy."

"Maybe you'd like to leave Little Leroy with me for safekeeping," Hank said.

Elsie retrieved the gun and tucked it into her bathrobe pocket. "I don't go anywhere without Little Leroy. Old ladies got to protect themselves. It isn't like I could give some guy a karate chop, you know. I don't move as fast as I used to. Sometimes I get arthritis in my knee when it's going to rain."

She turned and shuffled toward the stairs "I'm going to make myself a meat loaf sandwich. I always get an appetite when I get woken up in the middle of the night like this."

Hank pulled the shades on the windows and drew the curtains. "Where's Horatio? He was supposed to be sleeping in here?"

"He went under the bed when Elsie blasted that poor man off the ladder. I think he's still under there."

"Can't blame him," Hank said. "I don't know who's more of a threat—the guys that are breaking into this house, or Elsie and her cannon."

"Maybe we should call the police."

"I told Gordie Pickens about the first break-in. He's the sheriff for this part of the county. If I call him now, I'll probably wake him up. I'll file a report in the morning."

And tomorrow I'll go into town and see who's walking with a limp, he thought. Someone would be sore from falling off that ladder.

"This is too much of a coincidence," Maggie said. "Someone's after the diary."

"Have you got the diary in a safe place?"

"Between my mattress and box spring."

Hank stretched out on the bed. "Good. Then I can stay right here and protect you and the diary, all at the same time."

Maggie squinted at him in the darkness. "And who's going to protect me from you?"

"You don't need any protection from me. I'm doing my hero thing tonight. I'm going to stay by your side and keep you safe."

"To tell you the truth I don't think I'm in too much danger. These people don't seem very bright to me. I don't think we're dealing with hardened criminals."

"Yeah. Their second-story skills are definitely lacking."

"You think it could be a prank? You know, someone's idea of a joke?"

"Hard to believe. Even in my most rebellious stage I never did breaking and entering. Anyway, whatever the motive, I think Elsie did a pretty good job of discouraging them."

"Then why are you staying here?"

"I don't want to pass up an excuse to crawl into bed with you." He reached out and pulled her snugly against him. "How's this? Is this comfortable?"

"Actually . . ."

"Good," he said, wrapping his arms around her. "We can look at this like a trial run. This is how we'd sleep if we were lovers, but of course, we wouldn't have any clothes on. You'll have to use your imagination about the clothes," he whispered into her hair.

"Don't start."

"It was just something I thought I should bring to your attention. Details are important, you know."

"Uh-huh."

He threw his leg over hers and curled his

hand around her rib cage. "Can you imagine how my hand would feel on you if you were naked?"

"You're doing it again! You're trying to seduce me!"

"I know. I'm a scourge."

"You told me you were going to be a hero tonight."

"Oh man, are you going to hold me to that?" He gave an exaggerated sigh. "Okay, you're right. I said I was going to be a hero, so I'll be a hero, but I want you to know it's damn hard being a hero. I hope you appreciate this."

"Are you going to sleep now?"

"Yes."

"Good."

They lay together in silence for some time. Horatio stretched under the bed; Fluffy curled in an old-fashioned rocker. Downstairs, a mantel clock ticked away the hours. The darkness was thick and velvety, the air heavy with the orchard smells that drifted through the open window.

Maggie felt Hank relax, heard his breathing turn slow and steady. He was asleep. This was something else she could easily get used to, she decided. She liked this quiet part of sleeping with a man. She liked the warmth and security, the silent companionship. She was an extravagant personality, but she enjoyed the small pleasures of life the best. She liked to watch her cat stretch, liked to lick the beaters when she made whipped cream, liked the way Hank's arm felt as it possessively draped across her.

She lay there for a while longer, absorbing the pleasure of Hank's nearness, and little by little a different sort of pleasure stole into her. Little by little desire pushed the contentment aside and wanting took over. The wanting burned behind her skin and ached deep in her loins. She had never wanted like this before. Not with this unrelenting intensity. Not from simply being next to a man.

She moved against him; pressing her lips to his heated flesh. Her hand slid along the muscle-hard plane of his belly. Her breasts weighed heavy on him. She felt him stir, sensed a change in his breathing.

"Hank," she whispered in the darkness, her lips skimming lower. "About this hero thing . . ."

He groaned.

Her hand was splayed over his navel, and she could feel the muscles tense under her palm. Her own stomach responded with an equally strong contraction. So this was what it was all about, she thought. She'd never understood before. She'd never before been caught in the undertow of desire, never felt the pull of it.

His hands tensed at her back. "Maggie, what are you doing?"

"I think I'm seducing you. Is it working?"

Another groan.

"I've never actually seduced anyone before."

"Maybe you'd better think about it."

"Oh Lord, am I doing it wrong?"

"No! I just want to make sure this is what you want."

What she wanted? She was beyond wanting. At the moment loving Hank seemed crucial to her existence. Loving Hank seemed as essential as breathing air. She answered by wriggling out of her nightshirt and tossing it to the floor.

Neither moved. Nothing was said. Their breathing was shallow and silent. And then suddenly there was only passion. It roared through them like a flash fire.

He yanked his jeans off and came to her needing more than he'd ever before needed from a woman. He kissed her hard and deep, sweeping the length of her body with his hand. Loving words and tender exploration were saved for other times. There was an urgency and a ferocity to this first lovemaking that was more exciting than slow expertise.

She arched her back and cried out.

Mine, he thought. My woman, my wife, my love. He put his mouth to her and brought the fever back to her body.

He was a man who gave freely and took hungrily. He felt her move under him, heard her cry out at the intensity of the pleasure, felt her contraction tighten around him.

"Maggie." He could hardly say it, hardly breathe for the fire that consumed him. He thought his heart would leap from his chest, and then they came together with an explosion of passion that left both of them gasping. When it was over, they clung together, trying to assemble their thoughts.

She was the first to find her voice. "Wow," she said.

Hank couldn't top that, so he picked her up with shaking arms and carried her across the hall into his bedroom. "Clean sheets," he offered. "This next time is going to be slow and thorough, and I don't want you to be distracted."

"Oh my God," she half-moaned, "you mean there's going to be a next time already?"

Chapter 7

Maggie stood in front of the bathroom mirror and took stock. Her hair was impossibly tangled, her eyes were bleary from lack of sleep, her cheeks rosy . . . and she had a foolish grin plastered to her face. Stop smiling, she told herself. You look like an idiot!

Five minutes later she emerged from the shower, squinted into the fogged mirror and rolled her eyes. She was still smiling.

"They're going to know," she murmured. "They're all going to know. And *he's* going to know."

That was the worst part. Hank Mallone was going to know he'd just given her the best night of her life. She wasn't quite sure why that bothered her so much, but she felt like a cat with its hackles raised. Defense mechanism, she guessed. The more she loved him, the more wary she became. Weird. Definitely weird, she decided.

She pulled a comb through her curls, dropped a T-shirt over her head, put on a pair of black jogging shorts, and checked the mirror one last time. The smile was still there.

Hank was stapling a new piece of screen across the door when Maggie came into the kitchen. He looked up from his work and chuckled when he saw the smile on her face.

The heat rose from her shirt collar and burned in her ears. Wonderful. Now she was blushing. She made a frustrated sound and took out a carton of orange juice from the refrigerator.

Elsie put a plate of scrambled eggs on the table. She stepped back and took a good look at Maggie.

"That's some smile you got on your face. Shame on you. You two hardly know each other. I tell you, in my day we didn't go around smiling like that until after we were *really* married."

"It's only a smile, for goodness sakes," Maggie shouted.

"Well at least you're finally getting some exercise," Elsie said. "I guess there's something to be said for that."

Maggie slanted a look at Hank. He was leaning against the doorjamb with his arms loosely crossed over his chest, and he had a grin on his face that was even sillier than hers. She cleared her throat and concentrated on her eggs.

Elsie added an English muffin to Maggie's plate. "I've got to go now. I've got an appointment to get my hair done. I've got a date tonight."

"Sounds serious," Maggie said. "You better watch out you don't wake up smiling some morning."

"It's different for me," Elsie said. "I can't wait around. Men my age are dying like flies." She straightened her dress and took her purse from the kitchen counter.

"That's a pretty big purse," Hank said. "It looks heavy."

"It's not so bad," Elsie said. "Keeps me in shape. All the young women today go to them expensive spas with those fancy machines. I just carry a good-sized purse. I've got muscles in my arms those women only dream of."

Hank poured himself a cup of coffee and listened to Elsie gun the Caddy down the driveway. "There's only one thing I can think of to make that purse so heavy."

Maggie grimaced. "You checked her references, didn't you? I mean, she doesn't have a criminal record or anything, does she?"

Bubba opened the newly repaired screen door. "Howdy," he said. "Am I too late for breakfast?"

Hank looked at the kitchen clock. "Oversleep?"

Bubba cracked six eggs into the frying pan and poured himself a cup of coffee. "It's Saturday. I've been fishing. Ruben Smullen told me Goose Creek below the trestle bridge was doing real good, so I went out first thing this morning."

"Catch anything?"

"Got a mess of trout. They were just about standing in line to get on my hook. I got them in a cooler on the back porch. I'll split them with you."

He found leftover meat loaf in the refrigerator and added some slices to the pan. When it was cooked to his satisfaction, he turned the eggs and the meat onto a plate and covered it all with ketchup.

"That's a lot of breakfast," Hank said. "Even for you."

"I'm a man with a problem. I'm lacking

essential gratifications. So I'm substituting food."

"Does it work?"

"No."

"What's the problem?"

"Peggy wants to get married. Says there's not going to be any more . . . you know, until we get married. I blame you for this. You did it. It's like a disease. An epidemic. A plague. Ever since you got married, every woman for fifty miles is out to get a ring put on her finger."

"Maybe you'd like being married," Hank said. "You've been going with Peggy for years. Maybe it's time to get married. You aren't getting any younger, you know."

"Or any slimmer," Maggie said, watching him fork into his eggs.

"I don't know. The idea gives me the willies." He looked up at Hank. "You like being married?"

"Yup."

He shifted his attention to Maggie and grinned. "I can tell you like being married." He winked at Hank and leaned across the table to him. "Only one thing puts a smile like that on a woman's face."

Maggie stuffed an entire muffin into her

mouth and chewed. She'd agreed to stay for six months. She'd already been here for five days. That left 179 days. 179 breakfasts with Bubba. It wasn't an appealing prospect. She swallowed the muffin and washed it down with half a cup of coffee. "I have to go to work," she said.

"It's Saturday," Hank said. "Why don't you work for half a day, and we'll go for a drive. I'll take you up to the top of Mt. Mansfield on the ski lift."

Bubba looked up from his meat loaf. "You can't do that. You told Bill Grisbe you'd take a look at his Ford. Hank is a mechanical wizard," Bubba told Maggie. "And then we've got a game against West Millerville."

"Softball," Hank explained. "I forgot. Maybe we could go to Mt. Mansfield tomorrow."

"I thought you were going to Burlington with me tomorrow," Bubba said. "We were going to take a look at the new press Sam Inman just installed."

"Oh yeah. It's a great press," he said to Maggie. "It's the kind I want. He's got a thirty-two inch hydraulic rack-and-cloth press with a sanifeed unit."

Maggie felt her smile fading. Hank didn't have the time or the desire for a real wife. That was why he'd hired one. Lord, she was such an idiot. After their wonderful night, now she was playing second fiddle to Bill Grisbe's Ford. Men!

"Wouldn't want to disappoint Bill Grisbe," she said frostily. "And I certainly wouldn't want the softball team to do without you."

"Uh-oh," Bubba said to Hank. "I think she's mad. I think she's getting the old ball and chain ready to clamp onto your ankle."

Old ball and chain? Maggie felt the fire burning in her scalp, felt her temper kick in.

"Listen, Mr. Lard, it's none of your business what I clamp onto my husband's ankle. And for your information, your days are limited at this breakfast table. If you haven't dropped dead from clogged arteries by Wednesday, you're going to have to make other arrangements to fuel up." She glared at him. "Got that?"

"She sure gets riled," Bubba said to Hank. "Must be that book is wearing her out."

Maggie wheeled around and marched out of the room, shaking her head and muttering.

Hank grinned after her. "She likes me," he said. "She doesn't want to share."

"She sure is changeable . . . smiling one minute and calling me names the next. She's unstable, Hank. I'm telling you, the woman is loony."

Maggie stomped into her study and slammed the door shut. She wasn't loony, and she wasn't unstable. She was mad. Mostly she was mad at herself. She'd walked right into this with her eyes wide open, and now she was peeved because it was turning out just as she'd expected.

She threw herself into her chair and turned on her computer. Ignore them, she told herself. Concentrate on your work. Who cares about a silly trip up to the top of Mt. Mansfield.

She cared! She hadn't been off the farm for five days, and she was going bonkers. She cracked her knuckles and looked out the window. Apple trees for as far as the eye could see. Boring, stupid apple trees. They were always the same. At least her parking lot in Riverside had some activity. Cars going in and out. People taking their garbage to the dumpster. And then twice a week the big garbage truck would come and empty the dumpster. Now that was excitement.

She stared at the computer screen, rereading the last paragraph she'd written. She tapped a pencil against her forehead and pursed her lips.

"Now what?" she said. "Now what?"

She didn't know. She'd lost her momentum. She thumbed through the diary, but it didn't inspire her. So, Kitty Toone had become a madam to buy baby cereal.

"Big deal," Maggie said. "Everybody has problems. Look at me. I've got problems."

By two o'clock she'd organized her sock drawer and her lingerie, she'd written a letter home to her mother, she'd yanked the hairs out of her legs with hot wax, she'd put two coats of bright crimson lacquer on her nails, and she'd gone through two giant bags of potato chips. But she still hadn't typed anything into the computer.

She was lying spread eagle on the floor, supposedly thinking, but actually taking a nap, when she heard a car pull up in front of the house. She went to the window and watched while Hank's parents got out and made their way to the door. A surprise visit from her in-laws. They probably came to see if she'd set any more of the ancestral home on fire.

She took stock of herself and decided she looked utterly disreputable in her most comfortable but oldest shorts and faded T-shirt. Her hair hadn't been combed since before breakfast, and she'd lost track of her shoes. Maybe she could hide in her room, she thought. Maybe Elsie would answer the door and tell the Mallones that Hank was off with Bubba fixing somebody's broken-down car. Then, hopefully, they'd leave.

She heard Elsie move to the door when the bell rang, and she crossed her fingers. She really didn't want to face Harry Mallone.

There was the muffled sound of conversation in the foyer, and then Elsie yelled up the stairs. "It's the Mallones, Maggie. They came to say hello."

Maggie groaned. She ran an ineffective hand through her hair and took a deep breath. "Here goes nothing," she said, opening the door to her study.

Horatio bounded in. He put his paws on Maggie's chest and gave her a big, happy slurp on the face. He saw Fluffy sleeping next to the keyboard and did the same to Fluffy. Fluffy reacted with a lightning fast swipe that caught Horatio on the side of the head. Horatio yelped. He regained his footing, raised his hackles, and barked in the cat's face. "*Woof!*" Fluffy took off with the dog in pursuit.

Maggie ran down the stairs after them, stopping short when she reached the foyer. The cat was now affixed to Hank's father's chest.

Harry Mallone's face was brick-red, his even, white teeth clenched, his eyes bulged slightly. "This house is a loony bin," he said. "And I *hate* cats!"

Helen Mallone patted her husband's arm. "I think she likes you, dear," she said. "Remember your blood pressure." She smiled pleasantly at Maggie. "We were out for a drive and thought we'd stop around to say hello."

Maggie unhooked the cat claws one by one. "I'm terribly sorry!"

Elsie was still holding the front door open. "I've never seen anything like it. That cat just flew through the air to old Harry here. Must have some squirrel in her. She just flew through the air."

Hank's pickup rattled down the driveway and stopped in front of the house. Hank and Bubba got out and jogged to the porch.

"What's going on?" Hank asked.

"Your parents came over to visit, and the cat from hell attacked your father," Elsie said.

"That cat's a killer," Harry Mallone said. "It's a threat to society. It should be locked up, put to sleep, have its claws ripped out."

Maggie clutched Fluffy to her chest. "Over my dead body!"

Harry didn't look upset about that possibility. He raised an eyebrow and said, "Hmmmm."

Hank gave his mother a kiss on the cheek. "It's great to see you guys, and I'd like to stay and chat but I'm late for a softball game. Maybe you could stop by the field and watch me destroy West Millerville."

"That would be lovely," Helen said sweetly. "We could swing by Dr. Pritchard's office and get a tetanus shot for your father, and then we'll watch you play for a little while."

Hank took his cleats from the hall closet, rumpled Maggie's hair, and kissed her on the nose. "See you at supper. Don't forget about the dance tonight."

Bubba's mouth fell open. "You're taking her to the dance at the grange? You hate that kind of stuff."

"I'm going to the dance too," Elsie said. "I hear everybody'll be there. I even got my hair done."

"The grange holds two dances," Bubba told her. "One at the beginning of the county fair and one at the end of the county fair. This here's the one at the end of the county fair, and it's always the best. The king and queen of the fair will be there. One year Hank was supposed to be king of the fair, but he never showed up." He elbowed Hank. "Remember that?"

Hank's father shook his head.

"He was a trial," his mother said. "But now he's all settled down. Married to a lovely girl. No more crazy schemes. Goodness, it makes a mother feel good."

Maggie put her finger to her eyebrow.

"Something wrong, dear?" Hank's mother asked.

"A slight twitch. It's nothing. The doctor says it's a nervous disorder, but you can't believe everything those doctors say. I'm not a nervous sort of person. I'm really very calm. Don't you think I'm calm, Hank?"

"I told you she was loony," Bubba whispered to Hank. "You'd better watch her. Old Bernie Grizzard started with a twitch, and now he's talking to doorknobs."

Hank put his arm around her. "Of course you're calm, sweetcakes. You've just been working too hard. You've probably got eye strain from too many hours at the computer."

"She works day and night," Elsie said to Hank's parents. "It isn't natural for a body to sit in front of one of those machines like that. It's no wonder she's so pale and twitchy."

Maggie gasped. Was she realty pale and twitchy? Maybe she *had* been working too hard lately.

Hank patted her on the top of her head. "Poor little girl. All work and no play." His mouth curved into a seductive smile. "We'll fix that tonight, won't we?"

There was laughter in Hank's eyes, and Maggie knew it wasn't directed at her. He was fond of these people, and he was tolerant of them. He found humor where she found pure aggravation. She liked him for that. And she liked him for his silent reassurances. His eyes told her that she wasn't the least bit pale. His eyes told her she was beautiful beyond belief, and the smile was frighteningly indecent. The smile also produced a flood of memories from the night before.

"We're gonna be late for the game," Bubba said. "We'd better get going."

Helen Mallone responded to her husband's

hand at her elbow. "We should be moving along too."

Maggie waved good-bye to the Mallones and watched Hank follow them down the driveway in his faded Ford. The sun had baked the moisture out of the dirt road, and a cloud of dust rose like a plume, marking the truck's progress.

Maggie stood on the porch until the cars were out of sight and the dust had begun to settle. Excitement fluttered in her chest like a wild bird. She was going to a dance tonight! With Hank! How could she have forgotten? Easy. She had a short memory these days, she admitted. For instance, she'd just forgotten she was supposed to be disenchanted with Hank as husband material. In fact, not so long ago she didn't even think he looked so great as friend material. Now here she was in a state approaching euphoria because he was going to take her to a dance.

She put her hand to her mouth and found the smile had returned. She wasn't surprised.

"Life is not simple," she said to Fluffy, taking her into the kitchen for a dish of cat food.

Elsie was one step behind them. "You know, if I was after those diaries, I'd come get them tonight. There won't be nobody home tonight. They'll be easy pickin's. You don't just leave them laying around, do you?"

"I hide them under my mattress."

"Amateur stuff. We got to do better than that. We got to find a real hiding place for them if we're all going out."

Maggie popped open a can of kitty tuna. "I guess you're right. I'll find a better place as soon as I feed Fluffy. You have any ideas?"

"I read a mystery story once where they hid diamonds in the refrigerator. I always thought that was pretty dumb, because every man I ever met stopped at the refrigerator first thing. I figure you got to put it in something a man would never touch. Like a basket of ironing. Or maybe you could get a false-bottomed pail for the johnny mop."

"The diary is too big for a false-bottomed pail. It's actually seven books." She set the plate of cat food on the floor. "I guess I should hide my computer disks too."

"Tell me the truth," Elsie said. "Are those books worth stealing? Your Aunt Kitty know something the rest of us don't? She have trade secrets in those books?"

"I suppose there are a few trade secrets, but

I really don't think there's anything worth stealing. You can read them, if you want."

"Yeah? Maybe I will. I got some time off this afternoon. Maybe I'll just spend an hour or two browsing through them. Then we can find a good hiding place before we leave."

At six o'clock Elsie put dinner on the table. "I don't mind people not coming to the table to eat my food," she said. "You don't want to eat, you don't have to eat. But I'm not waiting dinner. Dinner is served at six o'clock, and if you want to eat, you'd better not be late. I don't care if the truck broke down or aliens landed on the baseball field, I'm not serving supper all night long."

An hour later Hank threw his cleats onto the back porch and ambled into the kitchen. "Smells wonderful in here, Elsie. I bet you made stew with homemade biscuits. I could smell it the minute I got out of the truck." He put his arm around her and gave her a squeeze. "I'm sorry I'm late. The game went into extra innings."

She gave him a narrow-eyed look. "Did you win?"

"Yup." He grinned down at her and pulled a baseball out of his pocket. "And I brought you the game ball too."

She slid the ball into her apron pocket. "Lucky for you I can be bought. I don't usually serve supper to people when they're late." She ladled out a plate of stew from the pot heating on the stove and added biscuits she'd had warming in the oven. "There's layer cake for dessert. You can help yourself. I got things to do."

Maggie was still at the table, lingering over a glass of iced coffee and a second piece of cake.

"How do you do it?" she asked Hank when he sat across from her.

"Do what?"

"Charm all the women. If I'd been an hour late, I'd be eating dry toast for supper."

"That's not true. Elsie would have saved supper for you. She's like a hedgehog. All prickles on the outside and soft and warm at the belly." He buttered a biscuit. "You weren't talking about just Elsie, though, were you?"

"No. I was talking about a lifetime of wrapping women around your little finger. Including your mother and me."

"I didn't realize I had you wrapped around my little finger."

"I'm resisting."

"Are we having a serious discussion?"

"Pretty much," Maggie said.

161

"Then we have to put all these women in the appropriate category. My mother doesn't count. Mothers spoil their children no matter how rotten they are. The girls I knew in high school were hardly wrapped around my little finger. When I came back home I was the bad boy returned, and every eligible female—and some that weren't—wanted to take a crack at reforming me.

"The truth is, that for the past five years I've allowed myself to be led around by the nose like Farmer Brown's prize bull, because it was the easiest thing to do. The only commitments I've made have been to the farm. And the only promises I've made have been to myself. I've been a safe companion for a whole flock of women who, for one reason or another, didn't feel ready to get married."

He finished eating his biscuit and took another. "And that leaves you. You're feeling sort of helpless because you're in love with me."

"I'm not!"

"Of course you are. It's only natural. Being in love is a debilitating experience." He should know, he thought. All she had to do was smile at him and he went to jelly inside.

"What makes you think I'm in love with you?"

"The signs are all there. You let me use the shower first this morning. Then you stood on the porch and watched me drive away this afternoon. And of course there's the smile."

"You think that's irrefutable proof?"

"A man knows these things."

Maggie licked the last bit of icing from her fork. "Okay. I'll admit that I'm infatuated with you, but that's as far as I'm going to go."

"Really sticking your neck out, huh?"

She wanted to tell him she had no intention of getting hung up over a man who preferred tinkering with an old Ford to tinkering with her, but she decided it wasn't a flattering comparison. So she took her empty cake plate to the sink and rinsed it. It gave her time to squeeze her temper back into its hiding place.

"Don't provoke me," she said. "I'm trying to whip myself up into a good mood for the dance tonight."

An hour and a half later she worried that she might have succeeded too well at that task. She'd spent an unusually long time in the shower, enjoying the feel of the warm water, while she thought about dancing with Hank. Now she was feeling *very* friendly. Friendly enough to want to look especially nice.

So she'd taken great pains to get her hair just right. She'd used a little blush, a swipe of apricot lip gloss, a smudge of eye shadow, and she'd applied a touch of perfume to strategic places. Maggie, she said to herself, you're wicked.

She wore a softly clingy black knit dress that molded to her breasts, was nipped in with a thin belt at the waist and had a full, swirly skirt. She considered it to be the most romantic dress she owned. It was one of those dresses that should have been boring with its high neck and simple lines, but on Maggie it was a knockout. The saleswoman who'd sold it to Maggie had swallowed and said it was flattering. Aunt Kitty would have approved.

Maggie was twirling in front of the mirror in her room, studying the movement of the skirt, when Hank knocked at her door.

"Maggie, are you alive in there? It's been hours since you got out of the shower."

"That's an exaggeration. It's been forty-five minutes." She opened the door and gave one final twirl for his approval. "What do you think? How do you feel about this dress?"

"You know how in cartoons they show this big thermometer, and the red column of mercury goes shooting up the glass tube and blows the top off?"

"Uh-huh."

His attention fixed on the full swell of her breast under the soft jersey. "That's how I feel about this dress." His gaze dropped to the cleft where the material seductively nestled into the curve of her thighs. "And I'm not taking you out in public until you put a slip on."

She looked down at herself. "Static cling." She shook the skirt out and spun around one more time. "There! Is that any better?"

Hank groaned. "There's no way I'm going to the dance with you wearing that dress."

"It's my favorite dress!"

"It's a threat to my mental health. And you don't want to know the physical effect it's having on me."

Maggie just looked at him and smiled a small feline smile.

It produced raised eyebrows and an

answering grin. "Maggie Toone Mallone, I think you're enjoying my discomfort."

"Nonsense," she assured him. "That would be mean." Then she laughed. Of course she was enjoying it. She'd never known such power. And she'd never known such excitement. It hummed against the fabric of her red silk panties and sent a hot flush to her cheeks.

"That giggle could get you into a lot of trouble, Maggie."

She liked the way his voice softened when his eyes grew hungry, and she considered that the dance might be dull compared to other activities that were available to her. A dangerous thought.

He ran a slow hand the length of her bare arm. "Elsie's already left."

"Hmmm. So, we're all alone?"

He made no reply. He just looked at her with such intensity that she imagined his passion had condensed—the way leaves eventually become part of the strata, decomposed into oil, compressed into coal, stressed through the eons into diamonds. She figured Hank was at the coal stages—hard as anthracite and ready to burn.

When he pulled her to him, she knew she'd been right about the hard part. In seconds the dress was spread in a pool of black at her feet. The lacy red scrap of a bra followed. His hands trembled at her waist, but his mouth was firm. Firm and hot and voracious. He hooked his thumbs into the bikini panties, and they were gone. So was Maggie's resolve to keep him at arm's length. He backed her into her room, and by the time they reached the bed, he'd stripped off his clothes.

"Don't think I'm trifling with you, Maggie Toone Mallone. This is all-out lovemaking," he said. "The kind that requires commitment." He gently pushed her onto the bed and covered her. "I expect you to make an honest man of me."

"I think it's too late," Maggie murmured.

"I'm talking about marriage, Maggie."

"Marriage? I thought we were talking about making you honest."

"That's just an expression!"

His hands were at her breasts, stroking across the tips, and she wondered why he was talking when this delicious heat was flooding through her. "Do we have to talk about this now? I'm having a hard time concentrating."

167

Hank decided that might be to his advantage. He supposed it was dirty pool to discuss marriage when she was in the throes of passion, but these were difficult times. And he was a desperate man. So he set about to disturb her concentration like it had never been disturbed before.

He moved slowly, using his body to exert pressure, teasing her with his fingertips, whispering words of love to her until she was wild and panting. She was almost on the brink, he thought, and he was almost at the point of insanity. He had to clench his teeth to momentarily stop the progress of his own passion. He'd been serious when he'd talked about commitment. He didn't want to make love to a fake wife. He wanted Maggie to be his. Forever. For really.

"Do you love me, Maggie?" He had to know. Had to hear it from her.

She could only blink at him. She wanted to tell him. Wanted to shout out her love, but her throat was tight and the words wouldn't come, so she nodded her head, yes.

"Will you marry me, Maggie?"

She licked swollen lips. "Really marry?"

He saw the flicker of doubt in her eyes, felt

the hesitation. He kissed her slowly, deeply. The restraint was costing him, but he continued the seduction. His mouth moved to her collarbone, caressed her breast and trailed kisses to her navel. She gasped and her eyes dropped closed, and he asked her again. "Will you marry me, Maggie?"

"Yes." Weren't they already married? They were living in the same house, sharing the same bed, exchanging smiles across the breakfast table. Marriage wasn't a piece of paper. Marriage was a condition of the heart. It was an attitude. Wasn't it?

Chapter 8

Maggie knew the smile was back. When the stars had finished exploding, when her heart had slowed to a normal beat, when that peculiar lethargy of after-loving had seeped into every muscle in her body, Maggie felt the smile return to her lips. She lay very still beside Hank and wondered how her body could be in such a state of euphoric contentment when her mind was such a mess.

Hank had proposed, and she'd said yes. It all had a dreamlike quality. Marriage had seemed perfectly natural fifteen minutes ago . . . now she wasn't sure.

Marriage to Hank meant marriage to Skogen, Vermont. It was an idyllic place for a vacation, but she didn't know if she could manage a lifetime of apple trees. And she didn't know if she could feel comfortable with the people. What if they were all like Bubba?

Hank was having second thoughts too. He was feeling guilty about having coerced Maggie into marriage when she was in a weakened condition. "About that proposal . . ."

"You took advantage of me."

"Yeah. You don't mind, do you?"

"Of course I mind!" Maggie propped herself up on one elbow. "Were you serious?"

"Absolutely. I love you. In fact, I'll ask you again just to make it official. Will you marry me?"

"I don't think so."

"Too late," Hank said. "You already said yes."

"I can change my mind."

Hank swung his leg over hers. "I suppose I'll have to wear you down again."

"What about the dance?"

"Wouldn't you rather get seduced?"

"No!"

He slid his hand over her belly and kissed her bare shoulder. "Liar."

"Everyone's expecting us to be there. What about your new image? What about respectability? What about the cider press?"

Hank groaned. She was right. He needed the cider press.

"Okay, we'll go to the dance. But when we get home, it's back to seduction."

Maggie put her hands to her head. "How bad is my hair?"

"Your hair looks great."

She sighed and got out of bed to look in the mirror. "Oh my God."

"You're not going to spend another three hours in the bathroom, are you?"

Half an hour later Maggie pulled the black dress over her head. She was wearing a slip, and her hair wasn't nearly as incredible as it had been the first time she'd arranged it, but she decided she was passable. The aftermath of passion had a tendency to lower her standards on these matters, she admitted. She followed Hank down the stairs and patiently waited while he locked the front door.

The light was fading rapidly. It would be dark before they reached the grange, Maggie thought. She climbed onto the bench seat of the battered pickup and winced at the twinge of excitement in her chest. How could she be nervous and fluttery about sitting next to a man she'd just made wild and passionate love with?

She'd always thought intimacy would breed boredom. She'd figured a romance was a lot like a fox hunt. It seemed logical that things would get a little dull after the fox was caught. Evidently she'd been wrong all these years. Now she compared romantic activities to eating peanuts. Once you got started, you were done for.

I must be strong, she told herself. She must fight this disease. She primly sat in the middle of the seat, resisting the urge to scramble next to him, when he slid behind the wheel. Her hands were clasped in her lap, her nose pointed straight ahead.

She wasn't dumb enough to think love could conquer all. No siree bob, she was going to take her time on a decision like marriage. Just because she *felt* married and *acted* married didn't mean she was going to sign on the dotted line. That was the one thing she'd been wrong about when she'd said yes to his proposal. That formal piece of paper called a marriage certificate really did make a difference. It was legally and mentally binding. It was scary.

"The grange is on the outskirts of town, by the railroad tracks and the grain silos," he said. "I hope you're not going to be disappointed. It's mostly just a big hall on the southernmost side of the fairgrounds. It's about the only place around to hold wedding receptions and town meetings, so it gets a lot of use."

He drove past the grain silos and the cold storage warehouse and pulled into the grange hall parking lot. It was already filled with cars and trucks so Hank parked on the grass.

"I hope you're up to this," he said. "I'm not much of a dancer. I'll probably step all over your feet. And folks are going to be gawking at you."

"I can handle it."

"And I'm probably going to have to knock out a few teeth and flatten a few noses to keep the men away from you and that dress."

Maggie looked down at the dress. "It's okay now. I'm wearing a slip."

"Honey, we'd have to cover you with full chain mail and armor to discourage men from drooling over you in that dress."

"Is that a compliment?"

"There might be one in there somewhere. Mostly it's a warning. Don't expect me to act like a rational person when Slick Newman tries to cut in on a dance."

The doors and windows of the barn had been

thrown open, and the thump of the band spilled out into the darkness. People shouted over the music, and laughter rose above it all. Inside the light was dim enough for romantic dancing but bright enough to see the details on Emily Palmer's new dress and the red highlights Laurinda Gardner had the beauty parlor put in her hair. Laurinda said the red highlights were natural, but Sandy Mae Barnes had been there when Laurinda was having her hair highlighted, and Sandy Mae had told Kathy Kutchka what she'd seen, and Kathy Kutchka had told Iris Gilfillan which was as good as telling the whole rest of the town.

Children somberly danced with the grown-ups, or sat sipping soda on the side lineup of wooden folding chairs that had been donated by the funeral home. Three little girls dressed up in party dresses chased a little boy across the dance floor. His face was flushed and white shirttails had escaped from his gray dress slacks.

"That's Mark Howser's kid, Benji," Hank said. "He's a real terror. He probably dropped a frog down Alice Newfarmer's dress."

"Do children always come to the dances?"

"Yup. If there's a wedding or a dance, everybody in town's invited and no one would dare stay home or they'd get talked about. There's no one left to baby-sit the kids, so the kids come too. The Christmas party is the best. Santa Claus hands out candy canes and coloring books, and Big Irma makes her famous eggnog. The Christmas party was the highlight of my life when I was a kid."

It was the PNA Hall transported to Skogen, Vermont, Maggie thought. There was the same dusty wood floor, the same raised stage for the band, the same cash bar in a separate room. Trestle tables and benches had been lined up on one wall, and a door led off to what she knew would be the kitchen.

It was Riverside all over again. But worse. She was even more of an oddity here, she realized. She and Hank stood in the doorway of the grange hall, and every head turned in their direction. "Good thing I wore a slip," she whispered.

He slung an arm around her shoulders and grinned down at her. "Feeling conspicuous?"

"This must be what it feels like to stand in the middle of the road at rush hour while you're naked."

"It's just that you're new, and Skogen's a little pressed for excitement."

"It's not just that I'm new," she said. "I'm *different*. I'm from New Jersey. I talk like I'm from New Jersey. I walk like I'm from New Jersey. Look at me! I even have New Jersey hair!"

Hank chuckled. "I don't think New Jersey should take credit for this hair. I think this is Maggie hair." He bent down and kissed the top of her head. "I love your hair."

"You think all these people know about Aunt Kitty?"

"I'd bet my life on it."

Maggie groaned. "Guilt by association. They probably think you married a loose woman."

Hank guided her through the crowd to the cash bar, muscling his way in front of Andy White and stomping on Farley Boyd's instep when he tried to approach Maggie.

"They just think you're sort of a celebrity since you're a writer."

Henry Gooley lurched in front of Maggie and winked. Hank lifted him three inches off the floor by his necktie. "You want something, Henry?"

"Urk."

"Put him down!" Maggie said. "You're choking him!"

Hank set Henry onto the floor and smoothed out his tie.

"Jest wanted to say howdy," Henry said, backing away.

Maggie closed her eyes and counted to ten. "This is fast becoming the most embarrassing night of my life, and considering the life I've led that's really saying something. You're acting like the village goon."

"Yeah. You bring out the beast in me."

Elsie elbowed her way through the crowd to Maggie. "This here's a humdinger of a party. I bet everybody for fifty miles came to this dance. I bet those guys who broke into our house are here." She patted her big black patent leather pocketbook. "I brought Little Leroy along, just in case."

"It isn't loaded, is it?" Hank asked. "I'd hate to see you shoot up the grange hall."

"Of course it's loaded. A woman's got to protect herself."

Slick Newman sidled up to Maggie. "Howdy," he said, "I'm Slick Newman and I was wondering if you'd like to dance."

Hank gripped Maggie's arm just above the elbow. "Elsie, you mind if I borrow your pocketbook for a minute?"

Maggie glared at him. "Don't you dare borrow Elsie's pocketbook." She turned to Slick. "I'd love to dance."

"Oh no, you wouldn't," Hank said, still holding tight to her arm. "You promised the first dance to me." He smiled amiably at Slick. "I'm a little tense tonight. I've never been married before."

"Sad," Slick said, giving him a consoling slap on the back. "You were one of the really great ones too."

Hank moved Maggie out onto the dance floor. "Okay, here goes," he said, assuming a dancing position. He took a deep breath and swayed a little. "How am I doing?"

"Good start," Maggie told him.

He held her closer and continued swaying. "Dancing isn't so bad after all. I think I'm going to like this."

"It'd be more interesting if we moved around some."

"I don't know—moving around sounds complicated." He eased her forward and stepped on her foot. "Oops, sorry."

"You'd better get the hang of this," Maggie said, "because I'm not marrying any man for real who can't dance."

"No problem. It's just a matter of timing. Oops, sorry." He carefully steered her around Evelyn Judd and Ed Kritch. "So, are you saying that if I learn to dance you'll marry me?"

"No. I was making conversation. I was providing incentive. I think I was teasing."

Evelyn Judd tapped Hank on the shoulder. "Is this Hank Mallone dancing? I don't believe it. Fifteen years ago we were named king and queen of the fair, and this bum misses my coronation dance! I know you're newlyweds and everything, but I think Hank owes me a dance."

Maggie stared openmouthedly as Evelyn deftly maneuvered herself into Hank's arms and glided away with him. Then she heard Evelyn gasp, and she heard Hank say, "Oops, sorry," and Maggie felt a little better.

"Guess it's you and me," Ed Kritch said.

He was tall and rangy with sandy-colored hair that fell straight down onto his ears and across his forehead. He held Maggie in a loose-jointed slouch as they traveled across the dance floor, making the usual inane dance floor conversation.

"How do you like Skogen?" he said.

"I like it fine," Maggie answered.

"The weather's been dry most of this week," he offered.

Maggie agreed.

There was a pause and they both knew he was working up to the big question. "I hear you're a writer."

"Yup," Maggie said.

"Is it true that your aunt left you her diary with . . . um, personal stuff in it?"

"My aunt was a madam, and while there are some personal observations, most of the diary consists of pretty mundane information."

They'd traveled halfway around the grange and were in the shadow of the open side door. "You mind if we stop here for just a second," Ed said. "The fresh air feels great."

Maggie momentarily turned her back to Ed and the door, taking the opportunity to look for Hank.

"Sorry to have to do this," Ed said. "Hope I don't mess up your hair none."

And then he snatched her out the door and threw a grain sack over her head. Her scream was cut short by a hand clamped over her mouth. She kicked out, but strong arms lifted her off the ground, carried her a short distance, and dumped her into a car.

The motor kicked in and the car jumped forward. Maggie was thrown off balance on a fast curve out of the parking lot, and then there was just the steady drone of the engine. Ed Kritch took the grain sack off her head and scooted to the farthest corner of the backseat.

"I hope this don't color our friendship since you're going to be living here for the rest of your life and we're practically neighbors and all," he said.

"You have to understand a million dollars is a lot of money. I wouldn't ordinarily consider kidnapping or stealing or any of that stuff. Last week Big Irma gave me too much change for a quart of motor oil, and I gave it back to her. The problem is, jobs are real scarce in Skogen. The only job I could get is pumping gas at Irma's, and it don't give me enough money to raise a family on. Evelyn and I want to get married, but we can't hardly afford it."

There were two men in the front seat. The driver did a half-turn and smiled at Maggie. "I'm Vern Walsh," he said. "Pleased to make your acquaintance."

He nodded to the large man sitting on the passenger side. "This here's Ox Olesen. Me and

Ed and Ox are gonna split the million three ways. Ox is gonna use the money to go to college to learn about computers, and I'm gonna buy a couple cows with it so I can start a dairy herd. See, we're not so bad, it's like Ed said, our roots are here in Skogen but we can't make any money here. We talked about it, and we figure borrowing your aunt's diary doesn't really hurt anyone."

Maggie shook her head in disbelief. Her initial fear and outrage were overwhelmed by her curiosity. "I can't follow any of this. What's this business about a million dollars?"

"Someone . . . I don't think we should tell you who, offered a million dollars for your aunt's diary."

Maggie felt the breath catch in her chest. "A million dollars? Why on earth would anyone want to pay a million dollars for Aunt Kitty's diary. I've read every word of it. It's not worth a million dollars."

"It is now," Ed Kritch said. "Hey, we could give you some of the money to compensate for taking you away from the dance. We aren't greedy. We don't need the whole million. We could divide it up four ways instead of three."

"I can't give up Aunt Kitty's diary," Maggie said. "She entrusted it to me. I promised to make it into a book."

"Bummer," Ed Kritch said. "We didn't count on that."

"The way I see it," Vern Walsh said, "is that your Aunt Kitty was a good old broad, and she'd probably like to help us all out. She'd be glad to know her diary was doing somebody some good."

He turned into the driveway and gunned the car down the dirt road to Hank's house. "If we get the diary real fast, then we can get back to the dance in time to see them crown the king and queen."

Maggie crossed her arms over her chest and narrowed her eyes. "I'm not giving you the diary. It's hidden and you'll never find it. And have you considered the consequences of kidnapping me?"

"We're real upstanding citizens," Ed said. "We've never done anything wrong before. We thought we'd just lie like the dickens and folks would believe us."

"Are you the ones who broke into the house last night and the night before?" Maggie asked.

"Nope. This is our first shot at it. I heard it was Lumpy Mooney who tried to get the diary last night. Word is he damn near broke his backside falling off the ladder."

Everyone but Maggie got a good chuckle out of that.

Vern stopped a few feet back from the house. Two cars were parked in the driveway, and the lights to the house were blazing.

"Well, will you look at this!" he said. "That's Slick Newman's car. And the piece of junk in front of it belongs to that runt-nosed Purcell kid."

"They're after the diary," Ed Kritch said. "Man, that really stinks. They broke right into Hank's granny's house. I tell you people in this town are going down the toilet. When I was a kid, you never had to worry about this sort of thing. You wouldn't think of locking your front door when I was a kid."

"So, what do you think?" Vern said. "You think we should get the sheriff?"

Ed chewed on his lower lip while he thought about it for a minute. "No," he finally said. "The Purcell family's hard up. Seven kids and old man Purcell's been gimpy ever since Maynard Beasley mistook him for a deer and shot him in the knee. Why don't we just go tell them it wasn't polite to break in when nobody was home. Then we can all look for the diary and divide the money up. Hell, there's enough to go around."

A car pulled up behind them. Everyone turned around to squint into the headlights.

"Probably Hank," Maggie said. "You'd better watch out. He'll break every bone in your body when he gets hold of you."

"Nah," Ed said. "It's not Hank. Hank drives a pickup, and these headlights are too low. Besides, Hank's a good guy. He'd understand about us needing the money."

The lights blinked off and several figures got out of the car. One of the men had a body slung over his shoulder. They approached Ed Kritch and looked in the window.

"It's Spike," Ed said, rolling down his window. "Hey, Spike, what are you doing here?"

"We got a hostage," Spike said. "We come for the diary and we got someone who knows where it is!"

Ed opened the door and Spike dumped Elsie into the backseat alongside Maggie.

"I'll never tell," Elsie said. "Not in a million

years. You could torture me, and I won't tell you."

"We don't know any torture," Spike said. "We were counting on you just helping out."

"They had me trussed up like a Thanksgiving turkey," Elsie said. "Brought me here in a flour sack. Can you imagine that? After I paid sixteen dollars to have my hair done too."

"It looks okay," Spike said. "And we washed the flour sack out last night so it wouldn't ruin your dress. We tried to think of everything."

"You'd need a brain transplant before you could think of *anything*," Elsie said.

Spike and Ed exchanged worried looks.

"What do we do now?" Spike asked. "How're we gonna get the diary?"

Ed ran a hand through his hair. "I don't know. Vern, you were in the army. You know any torture we could do on ladies?"

"I never learned how to torture ladies," Vern said. "You had to be in special forces to learn stuff like that."

"You should be ashamed of yourself for trying to terrorize a couple of defenseless women," Elsie said.

"Defenseless, hah!" Spike said. "You just

about broke Melvin Nielsen's knee when he tried to help me jam you into the car. And you got a mean mouth on you too. Shame on you for even knowing those words."

Elsie smoothed her skirt over her knees and set her black patent leather purse primly on her lap. "This has all been very upsetting," she said. "You don't mind if I get a hankie from my purse, do you?"

"No, ma'am," Ed said. "You go right ahead and get your hankie."

Elsie reached into her purse and pulled out the forty-five.

"Holy cow!" Ed Kritch said. "What the hell are you doing with a gun in your pocketbook? It isn't loaded, is it?'

Elsie squinted down the barrel at him. "Of course it's loaded, you ninny. And just because I'm an old lady, don't think I won't use this baby. I could shoot the eyelashes off a groundhog at forty feet."

Ed had his hand on the door handle. "Maybe you should put the gun away. You wouldn't want to hurt anybody."

"Justifiable homocide," Elsie said, pointing the gun at Spike. "You can't go around kidnapping old ladies and planning to steal personal property without paying the price. And besides that, you ruined my evening. I probably missed the hokeypokey. Looks to me like you deserve whatever happens."

Ed Kritch lunged for Elsie, knocking her arm aside, and the gun accidentally discharged in the scuffle. The noise rocked the car, and the bullet blew a gaping hole in the roof.

Ed Kritch, Vern, Ox, and Spike sat in stunned silence for a split second before letting out simultaneous screams and running for their lives. They all piled into Spike's car and took off down the driveway.

"Bunch of wimps," Elsie said. "I wasn't really going to shoot any of them."

Maggie pushed the hair back from her forehead with a shaky hand. "I knew that. I knew you were just putting a scare into them."

She took a deep breath and put her hand to her chest to make sure her heart had resumed beating. "What do you think we should do about the men in the house?"

Elsie put the gun back in her pocketbook and snapped it closed. "They won't find the diaries in a hundred years. We hid them real good. I say we go back to the dance, and if any of those guys makes a mess of the house, we get them to come back tomorrow and clean it up."

It seemed like a better solution than sending Elsie in there with her six-shooter blazing, so Maggie agreed. She slid behind the wheel and turned the key to the ignition. Now she had to decide what to tell Hank. He'd been ready to duke it out with Henry Gooley over a wink. He wasn't going to take news of a kidnapping calmly.

"I think I'll wait awhile to tell Hank about this," Maggie said to Elsie. "Maybe I'll tell him on the ride home."

"Good idea. I don't want nothing to ruin the rest of my evening. I've got a lot of dancing to catch up on, and I hear they serve coffee and cake at twelve o'clock."

Hank was waiting for them when they drove into the grange parking lot. "Where have you been?" he asked. "And what were you doing in Vern's car?"

Maggie just stared at him. She hadn't had the foresight to come up with a story.

Elsie shifted her weight from foot to foot. "It was me," she said. "I wasn't feeling so good."

Maggie nodded. "Yeah, Elsie wasn't feeling so good. So I took her home. We couldn't find you, so we borrowed Vern's car."

"But then when we got there I was feeling better, so we came back to the dance. Did I miss the hokeypokey?"

"Yeah," Hank said. "You missed the hokeypokey."

"Dang. What time is it? I didn't miss the coffee and cake, did I?"

"No. It's early yet. Coffee and cake isn't served until twelve." He watched Elsie hurry off to the hall before turning to Maggie. "Now, you want to tell me what really happened?"

"No."

"No?"

"I want to dance. You in the mood for a little cheek-to-cheek scuffling around?"

"I'm in the mood for an explanation."

"I can't tell you," Maggie said.

He narrowed his eyes. "Why not? What's going on?"

"If I tell you, you'll go beserk and spoil the dance. Elsie wouldn't like that because she's been waiting for the hokeypokey and the cake, I wouldn't like it because I'm not into violence, and then there's your new image to consider. Stable members of the community do not start brawls and trash grange halls."

"Why are you so sure I'd trash the grange hall?"

"Trust me on this one."

"I assume Vern plays a part in this. Not only did you come back in his car, but he's in the bar right now belting down booze like there's no tomorrow. Maybe I'll just go in and ask old Vern about this big mystery."

"Okay, I'll tell you, but you have to promise not to get violent."

"No way."

Maggie tipped her nose up a fraction of an inch and stuck her chin out. "Then I'm not telling you."

He looked down at the toe of his boot and swore vigorously. "You can really try a man's patience."

"You have to promise."

"I promise. But I'm not happy."

"It turns out half the town is after the diary. Someone has offered a million dollars for it."

"Get out."

"Cross my heart."

"It has to be someone from New Jersey,"

Hank said. "No one around here has that kind of money."

Maggie wasn't sure. There was something about the way Vern wouldn't tell her the name of the person offering the million dollars. She felt certain Hank could coax all sorts of information from Vern. And she was just as certain she didn't want to be around to witness the persuasion.

"Tomorrow you can do some sleuthing," Maggie said. "Tonight you have to dance with me."

Chapter 9

Maggie took her shoes off on the way home and tried to wiggle her toes. "They're dead," she said. "They'll never be the same."

Hank sat in a relaxed slouch behind the wheel. "It's your own fault. You insisted I dance with you."

"I was trying to keep you occupied so you wouldn't misbehave."

"I think you just wanted me to hold you in my arms."

There was some truth to that, Maggie admitted. He really hadn't stepped on her toes all that much, and he'd felt wonderful swaying against her in time to the music. In fact, she might have gotten downright carried away if it hadn't been so obvious that the entire town was watching their every move.

"So, what do you think of the good people of Skogen?" Hank asked.

"I'm not too impressed," she answered truthfully. "The men are all intent on stealing my diary, and at least half of the women are intent on stealing my husband. Big Irma warned me not to mess with your apple pie recipe. Mrs. Farnsworth told me I'd have a life of eternal damnation if I didn't take up quilting. And Clara somebody sneezed on my coffee cake."

"Clara Whipple. She has allergies."

"She did it on purpose!"

"Honey, Clara Whipple sneezes on everybody and everything."

Maggie rubbed her toes. "She should use a tissue."

Hank turned into the driveway and stole a quick look at Maggie's feet. "I'm really sorry about your toes. I tried to be careful."

"It's not your fault. You hardly stepped on my toes at all. I've been going barefoot so much lately that my feet aren't used to being in shoes."

Three cars passed them going in the opposite direction on the narrow dirt road. The last one was Bubba's. He stopped and rolled his window down. "Don't worry," Bubba said to Hank. "We made sure everything got cleaned up. We even left the porch light on for you."

"How thoughtful," Hank said. "I'll have to do something nice for you someday." He sat up a little straighter and got a bright look to his face, as if he'd just had a terrific idea. "I know . . . how about breakfast. Why don't you come to breakfast this morning?"

"I thought I wasn't supposed to do that anymore."

"This is a special occasion." He shot a look at Maggie. "You don't mind, do you, cupcake?"

"No bloodshed," she said. "I threw up watching *Rocky II*."

Hank waved good night to Bubba and continued along the driveway. "I thought people in New Jersey liked that kind of thing. And what about the time you hit that kid in the head with your lunchbox?"

Maggie didn't answer him. She was thinking about the diaries, hoping they were still safely hidden. Tomorrow Hank would make Bubba tell him the name of the person offering the million dollars. That would be a step in the right direction. They could go to the authorities and press charges, although the crime seemed vague. Conspiring to commit robbery maybe.

A million dollars was big time. If you wanted something badly enough to fork out that kind of money, you probably weren't going to be easily discouraged. When the locals failed to find Kitty's notebooks, it seemed logical that professionals would be hired, and professionals might be inclined to break kneecaps and shoot people if they didn't cooperate. In fact, she couldn't understand why a professional wasn't hired in the first place. If she were conspiring to steal something, she certainly wouldn't have told everyone in town.

"Hank, don't you think it's strange that someone offered a million dollars for the diaries and turned the offer loose on the Skogen grapevine?"

"Maybe it didn't start on the grapevine. Maybe the offer was made in private to an individual, and he didn't keep his mouth shut. Now everybody and their brother is running through my house looking for the good life."

He parked the truck and walked Maggie to the porch. He tried the door and found it locked. "Well, at least they locked up before they left."

A grim smile returned to his face. Only in Skogen would a pack of people break into your house and then lock up and leave the porch light on for you. And his best friend, Bubba, had been one of them! Obviously no one in Skogen considered breaking into Hank's house and stealing Maggie's diary to be a major crime. The truth is, it had more the flavor of a scavenger hunt or a fishing derby.

He wondered why. People in Skogen were responsible to a fault. They took pride in their town and took care of their own. There had to be a reason for them to feel they had license to get the diary. Greed was strong motivation, but intuition told him there was more to it.

Maggie watched him unlock the door. "How are they getting in? We locked the door and the windows when we left."

"This morning I had Melvin Nielson make extra keys at the hardware store. I imagine he made more than I requested, and now he's selling them."

"Oh, great. That makes me feel real safe. Is there anyone in this town who can't be bought?"

Hank pulled her into the dark house and closed the door behind them. "Never fear.

Horatio and I will protect you. And if we fail, there's always Elsie and the cat from hell."

She didn't need protecting nearly as much as she needed reassuring, she thought. As far as she could tell, everyone in Skogen was nuts. Generations of inbreeding, she decided. She looked at Hank and wondered how he'd escaped. He was a genetic masterpiece.

"Tell me about the people here," she said. "They aren't really as awful as they seem to be, are they?"

He hugged her against him. "They aren't awful, just eccentric. It's occurred to me that we take a lot of things for granted here because we're all so familiar with each other. And I've been thinking that my reputation might have something to do with the relaxed attitude folks have about breaking into my house."

"Tit for tat?"

"Something like that."

His words whispered through her hair, and she felt desire stir deep in the pit of her stomach. She had to admit she'd like to forget about Vern and Bubba and Mrs. Farnsworth. She'd like to go upstairs and spend the rest of the evening making love to Hank. If he could just give her some honest-to-goodness assurance that she'd be happy spending her life in Skogen, she'd race him to the bedroom.

And quite frankly at this point she might not even care if he lied. She was willing to grasp at anything that might justify another night of loving. She was a weak woman, she admitted to herself. She was a sad excuse for a headstrong redhead.

"Tell me the truth. Do you truly think I could be happy living in Skogen for the next hundred years?"

Hank thought that was a tough question. He didn't even know if *he* could be happy living in Skogen for a hundred more years. "A hundred years is a little unwieldy. Why don't we worry about the future in smaller increments of time?"

"How small?"

"Let's start out with the rest of the night." He kissed her just below the earlobe. "I feel fairly certain I can keep you happy for the rest of the night."

As usual Maggie was the last one at the breakfast table. She'd finally managed to roll out of Hank's bed, lured by the aroma of strong coffee and the sound of a heated argument going on in the kitchen below her. She hadn't gotten enough hours of sleep, but she felt fine. A little lazy maybe, like a cat with a full belly, sleeping in a sunny spot.

She ambled across the hall to her own room in search of clothes and a comb. Someone was stomping around the kitchen and shouting, but the words were muffled. Bubba was here, she realized as she tugged on a football jersey and a pair of running shorts. She tried to pull a comb through her hair, but it got stuck, so she gave up with an impatient grunt and told herself she preferred the tousled look anyway.

When she reached the kitchen, Bubba and Hank were standing toe-to-toe.

"I'm not gonna tell you," Bubba said. "It's not my place to tell."

Hank had him by the shirtfront. "You're supposed to be my best friend! I trusted you, and you broke into my house like a common thief!"

"If I'd found the diary, I'd have split the money with you. And it wasn't exactly breaking in. Slick had already opened the door."

"You were going to steal something from me!"

"Well, I guess it could look like stealing. On the other hand it didn't seem like stealing because—"

Hank tightened his grip. "Because what?"

"Oh, hell," Bubba said. "All right I'll tell you. Because it was your father who offered the reward for the diary."

"That's a lie," Hank said. "That's impossible."

Bubba shook himself loose. "It's true. He told Fred McDonough he'd pay him a million dollars if he could get hold of the diary."

"My father doesn't have that kind of money."

"Sure he does," Bubba said. "He's the president of the bank. He's the richest man in town."

It made sense, Hank thought. Ridiculous as it was, it made sense. It was the last piece of the puzzle. People were willing to steal the diary because not only would the diary remain in the family, but everyone trusted his father to do the right thing. His father's reputation was impeccable. Why his father wanted the diary was beyond his imagination: It was impossible to visualize his father making such an offer. His father wasn't exactly mob material.

"I'm going to straighten this out right now," Hank said. "I'm going to pay my father a visit."

Maggie poured herself a cup of coffee. "Say hello for me."

Hank clamped a hand on her wrist. "You're part of this family. You're coming with me."

"Oh no. No, no, no, no, no."

"Yes, yes, yes. It's your diary. You can drink your coffee in the truck." He grinned and squeezed her hand. "You look like you need it."

"Had a rough night," she answered.

Bubba cleared his throat. "I guess I'll go home now."

"No way," Hank said. "You're going to go get Fred and bring him over to my parents' house."

"Oh, man, Fred's not going to like that. Fred's going to be hungover. He doesn't have a woman to keep him in line," Bubba explained to Maggie. "Fred's not what you would call the catch of the town."

"You don't know of anyone else that's going to come looking for the diary, do you?" Hank asked.

"Nope," Bubba said. "I don't think there's anyone else left. Anyway, we searched real thorough, and we couldn't find it. Some folks are saying the diary doesn't exist. And most folks are afraid of your housekeeper."

He opened the driver's side door to his truck.

"I'll make sure Fred gets to your parents' house, but then I've got to go. I have to set the timing on my truck this morning. It hasn't been sounding right. Don't forget we promised to help clean up the grange hall this afternoon. And then there's the poker game tonight at Vern's house."

"You're awfully busy with community activities," Maggie said, sliding onto the bench seat of Hank's pickup.

Hank pulled her across his lap and kissed her. "Maybe I need to rearrange my social calendar now that I'm a family man." His hand stole under the football jersey and gently cupped her breast. He kissed her again; deeper, more passionately than before. "This beats the heck out of baseball," he murmured.

Her fingers fumbled with the snap on his jeans. "How about fixing Bill Grisbe's car?" She slid her hand along his flat belly until she found what she was looking for. "Does this beat fixing his Ford?"

His answer was an intake of breath and a groan of pleasure.

She wanted to tease him, wanted to take the role of the seducer, but as she curled her hand around him, she felt her body respond with the lovely heat and the delicious thrum of desire that his nearness always triggered. She forgot about wanting to tease, forgot they were on the front seat of a truck, forgot about everything but the man moving over her. He was knowledgeable now. He knew exactly where to touch, knew the rhythms of her passion, knew all her secrets, all her preferences. His fingers stroked her. His mouth devoured her. When she thought she was at her limit, he took her farther. Much farther.

Afterward they held each other close, both in awe of the power of their love, both wondering how they could have done such a thing in broad daylight, in the driveway.

Hank was the first to raise his head above window level. "No one watching," he said, obviously relieved.

Maggie felt like a silly teenager, except she'd never done this as a teenager.

Hank sat up and adjusted his clothing. "Okay, I'm ready to go see my father now."

"Maybe we should take showers first. Maybe I should comb my hair."

He cranked the engine over and stepped on the accelerator. "No. I want to get to the bottom of this."

Fifteen minutes later his parents were surprised to see him. "I didn't realize you got up this early," his mother said.

"Mom, I run a farm. I'm up at the crack of dawn every day."

"Yes, but you never got up this early when you lived at home. Have you had breakfast?"

"Yup. I've already eaten."

Helen Mallone looked at Maggie's hair. "A cup of coffee, perhaps?"

Maggie remembered the coffee she'd left sitting on the kitchen counter. "Coffee would be great."

Harry Mallone was at the table, reading the paper. He looked over the top of his half glasses and raised his eyebrows. "I didn't think you got up this early," he said to Hank. "Is something wrong?"

"Dad, I get up this early every day. I'm a farmer."

"Mmmm," Harry said. "Fancy apples."

Hank sighed and slouched in the seat across from his father. "Actually, something *is* wrong. People have been breaking into my house."

"I heard about that," his father said. "I don't understand it. We've never had that kind of crime in Skogen."

Hank stared coolly at his father. "Rumor has it, you're the reason people are breaking in. I heard you offered Fred McDonough a million dollars if he'd steal Maggie's diary for you."

Harry's first reaction was disbelief. His second was a smile that creased his face and produced a chuckle deep in his chest. "You aren't serious."

"I am serious."

Harry looked at him. The smile faded. "You *are* serious."

"The way I hear it, everyone in town is working nights, trying to make that million dollars."

Helen gave Maggie a cup of coffee and took a seat at the table. "Harry, did you do that?"

"Of course not," Harry said. "Where would I get a million dollars?"

"You're the president of the bank," Hank told him.

Harry looked appalled. "They think I'd embezzle a million dollars?"

Hank shook his head. "No. They think you're rich."

Helen reached across and patted Maggie's hand. "The people in this town are very nice," she said, "but you couldn't accuse them of being smart."

Fred McDonough knocked at the back door.

Bubba had been right, Maggie thought. Fred McDonough was definitely hung over. His eyes were heavily bagged and only half-open. He had the beginnings of a beard and under the beard his face was ashen.

Helen Mallone opened the door and gently curled McDonough's hand around a mug of hot coffee.

"I wish I were dead," McDonough said.

Helen clucked sympathetically. "You shouldn't drink so much."

McDonough looked at her like she was from the moon.

"We're trying to straighten out this stealing business," Hank said. "Did my father offer you a million dollars to steal Maggie's diary?"

McDonough took a gulp of scalding coffee and never blinked an eye. "Yep. He said he'd give a million dollars jest to get his hands on that diary. That was his exact words. I tried, too, but your damn dog liked to tear my pants' leg off."

Harry Mallone smacked his forehead with the heel of his hand. "Now I remember. That was a figure of speech, you idiot! I didn't mean I wanted someone to steal the blasted thing, I meant I was wondering about its contents!"

Maggie laid her hand flat on the table to steady herself, as relief washed over her in a dizzying wave. It had been a misunderstanding! She'd been sure someone had been after the diary to save face. She'd thought it might have been a misguided relative, hoping to protect Aunt Kitty. Or perhaps a former client worrying about his reputation. She'd even thought it might have been one of the local upstanding citizens, as preposterous as that might seem.

She took a steadying breath and sipped her coffee before questioning Harry Mallone. "Why didn't you ask to borrow it?"

Harry shrugged. "It was one of those things you say in a conversation. I don't really have the time or interest to read about the internal workings of a bordello."

Maggie felt herself stiffen at the insult. "Too bad," she said. "It's pretty interesting."

Harry gave her a severe look. "I bet."

"So, let me get this straight," McDonough said. "You never meant for me to steal the diary?"

Harry removed his glasses, folded them, and

placed them in the case on the table. "That's right."

McDonough stared off into space, clearly grappling with this new information.

Helen Mallone looked at her husband, her lips pressed tight together. "Harry Mallone," she said. "You've caused a lot of trouble. I don't usually interfere with the relationship between you and your son, but this is too much. You owe him and Maggie an apology, at the very least."

"It was an honest communication problem," Harry said.

"No," Helen told him. "There's more involved than that. You haven't had an open mind about him and his wife. Just look, he even gets up early now and eats breakfast."

Harry didn't look especially impressed.

"I think you should give him the loan," Helen said.

Color instantly rose to Harry's cheeks.

Helen sat with her hands folded together on the table, her eyes and mouth locked in unyielding determination. "I think it's the least you could do to set things straight."

Harry drummed his fingers on the arms of his captain's chair, assessing his wife's anger.

"He doesn't have the appropriate collateral."

"Baloney," Helen Mallone said, continuing to glare at her husband.

Harry rolled his eyes heavenward and threw his hands into the air.

By anyone's standards his mother was a flexible person, Hank thought, but when she truly set her mind to something, she was a woman to be reckoned with. Hank knew the only time his father ever threw his hands into the air in a gesture of futility was when he was forced to capitulate to his wife's obstinacy. Hank could count the times on one hand. The time his mother had insisted they drive to Ohio to spend Christmas with her sister. The time his mother decided to have the kitchen remodeled. The time Aunt Tootie had a hysterectomy and his mother had invited her and her dog, Snuffy, to recuperate in the guest room.

Maggie was in the middle of packing when Hank returned home from cleaning the grange hall.

"What's this?" he asked. "Why are you putting your clothes in these boxes?"

"I'm leaving. Your father agreed to give you the loan, so there's no reason for me to stay."

His thick black eyebrows drew together. "What do you mean, there's no reason for you to stay? I asked you to marry me."

"I don't want to marry you."

"You don't love me?"

"I didn't say that." Maggie stuffed a stack of T-shirts into her suitcase. "I said I don't want to marry you. I've spent too many years of my life in uncomfortable environments. I love my mother, but I can't live with her. And I can't live with you either."

"What's wrong with me?"

"Nothing's wrong with you. It's everything around you that's all wrong. Your father totally disapproves of me. Your best friend resents me. And your dog is mean to my cat."

"Is that all?"

"No, that's not all. I'm going nuts sitting in this room day in and day out staring at apple trees. I don't think I'm cut out for farm life. If I don't get to a shopping mall soon, I'm going to go into withdrawal. I want to talk to someone who doesn't say 'yup.' I miss the air pollution. I have a craving to stand in line and curse out someone. I miss being on the road and having other drivers make rude gestures to me."

Hank put his hand to her forehead. "You running a fever?"

"This town is filled with weirdos."

"Yeah, but most of them are pretty nice. You'd get used to Skogen if you just gave it a chance."

"Never!" Maggie said. "I will never get used to Skogen. I'm going back to Riverside, and I'm going to take a job at Greasy Jake's, and I'm going to finish my book. And then I'm moving to Tibet."

"Tibet isn't the paradise it used to be," Hank said. "I hear Tibet has problems too."

Maggie stuffed another stack of clothes into her suitcase. "Uh! No one ever takes me seriously."

"That's not true. I've always taken you seriously . . . until now. Now I'm not taking you seriously."

Hank picked the suitcase up and dumped Maggie's clothes out onto the bed. "We made a deal. The deal was that you would be my wife for six months. I expect you to honor that."

Maggie felt tears burning behind her eyes and angrily blinked them away. Why was he making this so difficult? It wasn't as if she really wanted to leave. She loved him. But some of the things she'd said were true. She thought she would be miserable in Skogen in the long term sense of things. And eventually Hank would be miserable too. And then they'd have a miserable marriage. And maybe by that time they'd have miserable children.

No, she thought, she didn't want to prolong the inevitable. She wanted to leave immediately and start to forget him. Didn't he understand that every moment in his presence was an agony for her?

"There's no reason for me to stay. You're just making things more difficult."

He set his chin at a stubborn angle. "We made a deal."

Her eyes were glittery with renewed obstinance.

"Okay," he said. "I live out in the barn for the next five months. Those are my terms."

She took on a defiant posture. "Fine. I'll stay. But don't expect me to like it. And don't expect me to cave in again. I intend to devote my energies to finishing my book. I'll perform whatever social duties you require, but don't impose your personal needs on me. Is that clear?"

"Perfectly."

Chapter 10

Maggie hung up the phone and sat back in her chair, staring sightlessly out her study window. It was early afternoon but the sunlight was weak, the world gray and obscure behind a curtain of falling snow. The orchard had been reduced to white mounds where snow had drifted from the last storm. The trees endured the cold in silence, reduced to skeletons beyond the sound of the muted footfalls and slamming doors that signaled life in the farmhouse.

It was the sort of snow people said would continue for a long time. Small, dry flakes that sifted straight down. Maggie knew a lot about snow now. Wet snow, dry snow, windblown snow, snow that was good for skiing, snow that was good for sledding, snow that was good for building snowmen. At happier times she would have been thrilled by it because she was usually a woman with an adventuresome spirit. But these weren't happy times.

Maggie was lonely in a house filled with people. She'd imposed it upon herself. She saw no other way. For five months she'd kept to her room, working day and night on Kitty's book. Hank had respected her isolation; Elsie had groused about it.

Now her tenure was coming to an end. Her six months would be complete in January. She'd accomplished her goal. She'd written the book. She'd even managed to sell it. Just minutes ago she'd spoken to her agent and learned she was a rich woman. Apparently she wasn't the only one who found the information in Kitty's diary to be interesting.

But the victory was flat. She was miserable. Cutting Hank out of her life had only produced heartache so strong that at times it left her breathless. Thank goodness the book had demanded her attention throughout most of her waking hours. Now that it was finished she was bereft.

She had to start a new project, she told herself, but nothing appealed to her. She looked down at herself and knew she'd lost weight.

"Pathetic," she said to Fluffy, curled in a ball on the corner of the desk.

Elsie knocked on the door and walked in. "Pathetic," she said. "Everyone's downstairs trimming the tree, and you're up here looking like death warmed over."

Maggie smiled. She could always count on Elsie to jolt her out of self-pity. Elsie was brutal but effective. And there'd been a lot of times in the past months when Elsie had kept her going with scoldings and hugs and hot soup.

"Tonight's the Christmas party," Elsie said. "Does your dress need pressing?"

Maggie shook her head. Her dress was fine. It was a little big on her, but the style allowed for that. She wasn't sure she cared anyway.

Laughter carried up the stairs with the smell of pine and spicy cider. Hank's parents, his Aunt Tootie, Slick, Ox, Ed, Vern, Bubba, and their wives and girlfriends were downstairs, helping with the tree.

If she were a good wife, she'd be down there too. She'd used the same tired excuse of working on her book to steal away to her room. No one knew the book was done, much less sold.

Lord, what had become of her? She was a

coward, she thought. She wasn't able to face other people's happiness. Especially now that it was the Christmas season. This was a time for family. A time for love—and Maggie was loveless. Tears trickled down her throat. Hormones, she told herself, swallowing hard.

Elsie shook her head and sighed. "You're so hard on yourself," she said. "Why don't you let yourself have some fun?"

Because if she gave in just a tiny bit, her resolve to leave would crumble like a house of cards, Maggie thought. Skogen wasn't going to change. Hank's father wasn't going to change. Bubba wasn't going to change. Just as her mother and Aunt Marvina weren't going to change. And the most painful truth was that Maggie wasn't going to change.

She didn't belong in Riverside and she didn't belong in Skogen. If she wanted happiness, she was going to have to go searching for it. Surely there was a place where she would be accepted and feel comfortable. Surely there was a town out there that offered a compromise between dumpsters and apple trees.

"I'll have fun tonight," Maggie lied. "I'll just work a little bit more, and then I'll quit for the day."

"Everyone misses you," Elsie insisted.

They didn't miss her. Maggie knew that for a fact. She could hear the laughter. She could hear the conversation that bubbled between old friends and family and never included her. For months now life had gone on in the farmhouse, and she hadn't been a part of it. Hank had gone from the baseball team to the football team to the hockey team. The cider press had been delivered and was operating, and the pie factory was close to becoming a reality.

"No one misses me," Maggie said. "They're having a perfectly wonderful time without me."

"Hank misses you," Elsie said. "He looks almost as bad as you do. He laughs, but his eyes don't mean it. You'd see it too if you weren't so stuck on your own misery."

Maggie wondered if what Elsie said was true. She knew part of her wanted it to be so. She knew that there was a scrap of hope she hadn't been able to completely smother. Her love for Hank smoldered deep inside her. She couldn't extinguish it no matter how hard she tried. It burned constantly and painfully. Every day she faced the unpleasant realities of her predicament and exerted every ounce of discipline she possessed to do what she felt was best for herself and for Hank, but the dream remained.

Deep in her heart she knew she hadn't held to the agreed-upon six months through any sense of honor. It had been that damn dream that had kept her in Vermont.

For weeks she'd been dreading the Christmas party at the grange hall. It was the one social event she couldn't possibly avoid. Now that it was at hand she felt numb and exhausted even before the ordeal began.

She sat on the edge of her bed with her bathrobe wrapped tightly around her. Her hair was still damp from the shower; her toes were pink from the hot water. A depressing lethargy had taken hold of her. At least she wasn't in one of her emotional moods, she thought. Lately she'd been succumbing to crying jags. No one knew. She cried quietly with her face stuffed into her pillow. She cried late at night when everyone else was asleep.

There was a soft rap on her closed door. "Maggie, can I come in?"

It was Hank. Probably wondering why she was so late. She should have been dressed half an hour ago, but she couldn't seem to finish the task. "The door's unlocked."

He wore a dark suit with a white shirt and red tie, and the corner of a red silk handkerchief peeked rakishly from his breast pocket. The sight of him made her heart feel like lead in her chest.

Hank Mallone would never want for female companionship, she thought. Once she was out of the scene, women would be flocking to his doorstep. He was sinfully handsome and in a few years he would be wealthy. The contracts for his pies and cider were pouring in. After the first of the year when the pie factory opened, Skogen would be at a hundred-percent employment thanks to Hank.

He sat beside her on the bed and placed a small paper-wrapped box in her hand.

"It's customary in my family to give a gift on the night of the Christmas party. When I was a little boy, my parents always gave me a special present just before we left. It would be something I could take with me. A pocketknife, or a pair of red socks, or Christmas suspenders. And my dad would always give my mom jewelry. I know this is hard to believe, but in his own way, my dad is actually quite romantic."

She hadn't expected this. Wasn't prepared for it. In the last two months they'd barely spoken, and she harbored a secret fear that he finally wanted her to leave. He'd stopped trying to make conversation, stopped finding excuses to touch her, stopped trying to coax her from her room.

And now he'd given her a gift. She didn't know what to make of it. She held it in her lap to keep her hands from shaking, but she wasn't entirely successful. Emotions too long held in check were tumbling to the surface, making it difficult to think, making it difficult not to smile.

For months now she'd treated him badly. And how had he responded to that? He'd bought her a gift!

He sat quietly watching, seeing the confusion in her face, seeing the pain mingling with a sudden infusion of unexpected joy. He'd been waiting for this moment for months, knowing that even if her book wasn't finished, even if all feelings for him were gone, she'd have to give him this evening.

He drew a shaky breath while she stared at the box. He hadn't been sure she'd accept it. He wasn't even sure she'd open it. Now that he saw the range of emotions play across her face, he knew things would work out.

He pulled her onto his lap and cuddled her close to him.

"I haven't wanted to bother you these past months. I know how hard you've been working on your book."

She thought she owed him an honest reply. "My book is done. It's been done for a little over a month now."

He understood her reasons for not telling him. She'd been using the book as an excuse to remain aloof. He'd suspected as much. He hadn't heard any computer noises lately. The slight hurt, but he struggled not to let it show.

"Can you tell me about it? Is it good?"

Maggie laughed softly. It was an odd question. It was like asking a mother if her firstborn daughter was ugly.

"I'm not sure if it's good, but it's sold. I've kept my promise. Aunt Kitty's diary will be published in book form."

He gave her a squeeze. "I always knew you could do it."

She liked the sound of pride in his voice, and it triggered a surge of pride in herself, bringing the first rush of excitement over her success.

"I wasn't that sure," she said. "I still can't believe it."

She was smiling. First with her mouth, then with her eyes, then every vestige of sorrow vanished. It was as if the sun had suddenly come out in all its blinding glory. Maggie Toone wasn't a woman who took easily to unhappiness.

She remembered the package, and her fingers fumbled with the wrapping paper. "I love presents!" she said. "I love surprises!" She opened the box to find a pair of diamond stud earrings. "Oh!"

He pushed a curl behind her ear so he could see her face more clearly. "Do you like them?"

"Yes! Of course I like them. They're beautiful. But . . ."

"But what?"

She slouched against him, some of the old tiredness returning.

"I can't accept these. This isn't the sort of present you give to a . . ." She searched her mind for the appropriate word, but couldn't find one that defined their relationship. "Friend," she finally said. "This isn't the sort of present you give to a friend."

"It's the sort of present I give to my *best* friend."

"I thought Bubba was your best friend."

"Bubba is my second best friend."

She thought he'd given up, but he'd only been lying low. She had to give him something for tenacity. And she had to admit—she was pleased. The dream was dancing around inside of her. She couldn't control it.

"It isn't going to work," she said. "Skogen hasn't changed."

He looked confident. "It'll work. It was never necessary for Skogen to change. You just haven't seen it yet. You haven't figured it out."

"I don't know what you mean."

"I was just like you. I had to get away. Trouble was that for a while my problems kept following me. That's because you can't run away from your problems. You only end up with the same problems in a new location.

"Then one day I was sitting in a crummy hotel room in Baltimore, and I realized I'd grown up. Somewhere along the line I'd sorted things out. My identity wasn't dependent upon the people around me. I didn't need my parents' attention or approval. I didn't need to be the class clown or the macho stud or the star quarterback. I just needed to do things I found personally satisfying. Like studying about agriculture, and improving my granny's apple orchard.

"I think you're a little like that. I think you needed to get away and write your book. And I think you needed some time alone to get in touch with Maggie Toone."

She shook her head. "I don't know if it's that simple. I don't know if I can stand the isolation of living on a farm."

"You've imposed your own isolation. We brought your little red car up here, but you haven't used it. You just need to get yourself out on the road. You need to cuss out a few old ladies, give a few rude hand signals. You need to hit those shopping malls once in a while."

"Vermont has shopping malls?"

"Mostly we have towns," he admitted. "But they're just as good as a mall. Burlington even has a pedestrian street. Doesn't that get your adrenaline going?"

Not nearly as much as sitting on his lap, Maggie thought. Still, it might be worth an investigation.

"And if you want to get out of the house on a regular basis, you could go back to teaching."

"No. I don't think so," Maggie said. "I think I want to write another book."

"Have you got an idea?"

She shook her head. "My creative energy hasn't exactly been at an all-time high."

"My Uncle Wilbur ran the county newspaper for forty years. He retired in 1901. We have crates and crates of papers in the basement of this house. I went down to check on them the other day. They're fragile, but they're still readable. Maybe you could find a new story in one of them."

Maggie's heart beat a little faster. Forty years' worth of old newspapers in her very own basement! It might be worth marrying Hank just for the newspapers alone!

Wait a minute. Hold the phone. She was getting carried away. Okay, so the Gap had come to Vermont and there was a book lurking somewhere in Hank's cellar. What about all those weird Skogenians who didn't like her? What about Bubba? What about Vern? What about Mrs. Farnsworth and her quilts?

Hank kissed her on the nose and set her on her feet.

"We need to get going. We don't want to miss Santa Claus. You go put your earrings on and finish getting dressed, and I'll warm up the truck."

Ten minutes later Maggie was sitting in the

truck, studying her earrings as they sparkled in the rearview mirror. She really shouldn't be wearing them, she thought. She hadn't intended to, and then somehow they'd managed to become attached to her ears. She wouldn't keep them, of course. She'd wear them to the dance, so as not to be rude, and then as soon as she got home, she'd swish them in alcohol and put them back in the box.

It would be different if she were legally married to Hank. It might even be different if she knew for sure about the shopping street in Burlington. Actually, now that she knew the shopping street was there, it didn't seem nearly so important to her.

She watched the last of the apple trees disappear from sight as Hank drove down the road, and she thought how pretty the trees were draped in snow and moonlight. She thought the town was pretty, too, when they passed through. Big Irma had strung outdoor lights around the general store, the bank was spotlighted with a green wreath on the door, the cafeteria and the beauty salon were trimmed in blinking lights, and the real estate office had decorated the fir tree in its front yard.

"Drive slower!" Maggie said, pressing her

nose to the window. "I can't see the decorations when you drive so fast!"

"I'm only doing twenty-five miles an hour. If I drive any slower, we'll be going backward."

She'd come back tomorrow to take a closer look at the Christmas tree, she decided. She wanted to see it in the daylight. And maybe she'd stop in at Big Irma's and buy some maple syrup candy to send to New Jersey.

In a matter of minutes they were at the grange hall, and it might as well have been the PNA. Halls are the same the world over, Maggie concluded. There was the same wonderful dusty wood floor, the same happy pandemonium of excited children and convivial adults. And because this was a Christmas party, there was a feeling of expectation. Santa would soon be here. And after Santa had handed out the candy canes and coloring books there would be dancing, and after the dancing there would be the special coffee cake made by the Smullen twins.

Maggie handed Hank her coat and looked into the crowd. "Oh, look," she said, "it's Vern! In a tuxedo!"

"Yeah, Vern always wears a tuxedo to the Christmas dance. He inherited it from his Uncle Mo."

"What happened to his Uncle Mo?"

"Heart attack," Hank said. "He was a waiter at a fancy restaurant in Burlington. That's where the tuxedo came from."

Vern winked at Maggie and she waved back.

Ed Kritch came over. "You be sure and save a dance for me," he said to Maggie.

Maggie looked at him suspiciously. "You won't kidnap me again, will you?"

Ed chuckled. "Naw, I wouldn't do that. That was something, wasn't it? I tell you, I just about fainted myself when Elsie Hawkins pulled that bazooka out of her purse. Yes sir, I guess that story's gonna get told around. I guess that's almost as good as the time Bucky Weaver burned his barn down trying to shoot Hank here."

Hank looked pleased. "Before you came into my life, I was the sole source of entertainment for this town," he said to Maggie. "It's a real pleasure to share the limelight."

A Christmas tree had been placed in the middle of the dance floor and a ring of people began forming around the tree. The band played "Here Comes Santa Claus" and the people sashayed around the tree in time to the song. Hank and Maggie joined hands and sashayed around, too, looking over their shoulder, watching the front door for the arrival of Santa Claus.

The door opened and Santa appeared, and every child in the hall sent up a squeal of delight.

"Ho, ho, ho," Santa said, joining the party. "Has everyone been good this year?"

"Yes," they all answered.

Dancing continued around the tree, and Santa made his way along the chain, talking to children, passing out his coloring books. When Santa got to Maggie, he stopped and took her hand.

"Has Maggie been good his year?" he asked.

Maggie felt her face flame. Santa hadn't talked to any of the other adults.

Santa took a coloring book and a candy cane from his sack and gave it to Maggie. "Only the best girls in Skogen get these," he said to Maggie with a wink.

A roar of approval went up from the crowd.

The world blurred for a moment, and Maggie's feet forgot to move to the music. She looked first to Hank and then to the other faces in the chain. They liked her! Maggie realized. Even Hank's father was smiling at her from across the room.

Maggie clutched the coloring book and the candy cane to her chest and dutifully thanked Santa. She took a good look at the man behind the beard and narrowed her eyes.

"I know it's you, Bubba," she whispered. "I'm gonna get you for this!"

Bubba smiled, gave Maggie's hand a squeeze, and moved on.

Maggie smiled after him. She smiled because all of a sudden she liked Bubba very much. And she smiled because Santa had found her, way out in the rolling, snow-covered hills of Vermont—and he'd given her a coloring book. She was blinking furiously, but the tears were spilling down her cheeks. She buried her face in Hank's chest and snuffled into his tie.

"It's just that I l-l-love coloring books," she said, sobbing.

Orville Mullen was on the other side of Maggie. "Probably pregnant," he said to Hank. "That's the way they get. They cry over coloring books and baby bibs and little booties. When my Elaine was pregnant, we couldn't walk past the baby food jars in the Acme without Elaine bursting into tears."

Mrs. Farnsworth came over and put her arm around Maggie. "You need to do some quilting," she said. "It evens a person out. And you get to gossip too."

"I don't know . . ." Maggie said, blowing her nose in Hank's red silk handkerchief.

"Doesn't take much time at all," Mrs. Farnsworth told her. "A Saturday afternoon once a month, and you can tell us about your Aunt Kitty's diary. We're all dying to read the book when it comes out. It's not every day we get a real author moving into our town. Maybe we can even hold a book-signing party."

A book-signing party? Maggie clapped a hand to her mouth to stop the giggles. She was going to be famous. Not enormously famous, of course. After all, she wasn't Nora Roberts. Still, she'd be a little famous. And the quilting club would give her a book-signing party. Maggie chewed on her bottom lip. She had a problem. A name problem.

"You're going to have to marry me as soon as possible," Maggie said to Hank. "I have a name problem. When the quilting club gives me a book-signing party, what am I going to write? They think I'm Maggie Mallone when actually I'm still Maggie Toone. You see, it will be much too confusing unless we get married right away."

She chewed on her bottom lip. "I realize it's been several months since you asked me to marry you. Maybe you've changed your mind. I couldn't blame you if you have."

Hank grinned down at her. "Let me get this straight. You want to marry me so you can autograph copies of your book for the quilting club?"

"Yes."

He couldn't resist teasing a little. "I don't know. That's not very romantic. I'm not sure that's a good reason for marriage. What about Skogen? You sure you can live here?"

"Of course I can live here! Skogen's a terrific place to live!" Her voice turned lower, more serious. "And I love you."

He took her in his arms. "I love you too. And I'll be happy to marry you." Then he kissed her long and hard. Right there in front of the whole town for everyone to see.

"Nice to know he's not doing it in people's barns anymore," Gordie Pickens said. "He sure was something as a youngster, wasn't he?"

Bucky Weaver, old Dan Butcher, and Myron Stonehouse agreed.

And the band played "Rudolph the Red-Nosed Reindeer" for the fourth time.

Enter the World of Janet Evanovich
Don't miss any of her early romances!

The Rocky Road to Romance

Her tall, dark, and deliciously dangerous
boss . . .

When the delightful, daffy Dog Lady of
station WZZZ offered to take on the
temporary job of traffic reporter, Steve Crow
tried to think of reasons to turn Daisy
Adams down. Perhaps he knew that sharing
the close quarters of a car with her for hours
would give the handsome program director
no room to resist her quirky charms. He'd
always favored low-slung sports cars and
high-heeled women, but that was before he
fell for a free spirit who caught crooks by
accident, loved old people and pets, and had
just too many jobs!

Loving Daisy turned Steve's life upside down,
especially once he adopted Bob, a huge dog
masquerading as a couch potato. But was
Daisy finally ready to play for keeps?

Love Overboard

Sinfully handsome schooner captain Ivan Rasmussen deserved to be called Ivan the Terrible, Stephanie Lowe decided. First, he sold her a haunted house, and now he was laughing at her Calamity Jane cooking! She only agreed to work one voyage of his Maine coastal cruise in exchange for the house repairs promised by her cousin, who'd run off to marry a plumber.

But the brazen Ivan, descendant of a pirate, insisted on flirting with her. When the voyage ended, he even managed to be on hand to help her trap the "ghost" in her house. Fun and comic mayhem, as only Janet Evanovich can write it.

Back to the Bedroom

For months he'd thought of her as the Mystery Woman, draped in a black velvet cloak, with outrageous red curls, flawless skin, and carrying a large, odd case. But the night David Dodd sees a helicopter drop a chunk of metal through the roof of his lovely neighbor's bedroom, he gets to meet the formidable and delightful Katherine Finn at last!

Kate is a driven concert musician with more commitments than hours in the day. Dave is a likable slacker who seems to be drifting through life. Yet no one has ever made her feel as cherished, and she's never had so much fun, even though her eccentric boarder, Elise, assures her that where Kate is concerned Dave has plenty of ambition.

Manhunt

Alexandra Scott, Alaskan Wilderness Woman. It had a terrific ring to it, but Alex felt a sudden twinge of uncertainty. She'd traded in her Wall Street job and fancy condo for a rundown cabin in the woods and a bait-and-tackle store. She'd wanted to escape the rat race and go husband-hunting where men outnumbered women four to one, but was she ready for the challenge?

Then she spotted Michael Casey, a sexy pilot who was undaunted by disaster, had hero written all over him . . . and was a confirmed bachelor. Michael Casey was the man she had come to Alaska to hunt, and Alexandra Scott had him in her sights.

Smitten

Single mom Lizabeth Kane wasn't exactly construction-worker material, but she truly wanted a job—and Matt Hallahan found her radiant smile utterly irresistible. When he agreed to hire her as a laborer, Lizabeth sent up a cheer. Since her divorce from a snobby philanderer, she'd frankly lost interest in men, but this macho carpenter, who smelled of sawdust and musk, made her senses sizzle.

As for Matt, he was charmed by Lizabeth's enthusiasm, her spunky kids, and wacky aunt. Clearly this was a match made in heaven.

Thanksgiving

When Megan Murphy discovers a floppy-eared rabbit gnawing on the hem of her skirt, she means to give its careless owner a piece of her mind—but Dr. Patrick Hunter is too attractive to stay mad at for long.

As for Patrick, he wants to play house together and make Thanksgiving dinner for their families. But Megan has wept over one failed love and is afraid to risk her heart again.

Wife for Hire

Hank Mallone spotted trouble when she sat down and said she'd marry him. Maggie Toone was a tempting firecracker who'd make his life delightful hell if he let her pretend to be his wife in order to improve his rogue's reputation. Would his harebrained scheme to get a bank loan for his business backfire once Maggie arrived in his small Vermont town and let the gossips take a look?

Maggie never expected her employer to be drop-dead handsome, or to affect her like a belt of bourbon on an empty stomach, but she was too intrigued by his offer to say no . . . and too eager to escape a life that made her feel trapped. The deal was strictly business, both agreed, until Hank turned out to be every fantasy she'd ever had.